A Little Thing Called Love

A Little Thing Called Love

A MARRYING THE DUKE NOVELLA

CATHY MAXWELL

AVONIMPULSE
An Imprint of HarperCollinsPublishers

Excerpt from *The Match of the Century* copyright © 2015 by Catherine Maxwell, Inc.

EPub Edition SEPTEMBER 2015 ISBN: 9780062407719
Print Edition ISBN: 9780062407726

10 9 8 7 6 5 4 3 2 1

For Andrew and Holly
May you set the world on fire.

Chapter One

London 1780

"HAVE YOU TAKEN leave of your senses, man? Do you know who she is?"

Fyclan Morris shrugged off his friend John Bishard's astonished questions. "She's a goddess," he replied, moving after the heavenly creature who had passed them as they had come out of the watchmaker's shop.

The young woman, a vision in blue ribbons and lace from the top of her pert brimmed bonnet to the trim of her hems had not noticed him, as a proper young woman should not. Accompanied by a manservant and maid, she'd weaved her way through the crowded street, her attention on a piece of paper in her hand, unaware that she'd changed his life forever.

It was *her*. Fyclan did not doubt the fact.

"*You'll recognize her immediately,*" his Gran had said. "*She'll be fair to your dark, a light to your step, a force you will not deny.*"

His Gran had claimed to see the future. She saw it in dreams, she said. The Irish believed in prophecy and accepted what they could not understand, but even among them, his Gran's gift was special. She was Romany-born, a gypsy until the day Fyclan's grandfather claimed he'd woven moonbeams into a rope and captured her to keep her.

Fyclan had never doubted the story. There *had been* something magical about her. She had a knowledge of things that no one could explain. Even the priest claimed to be puzzled, and it was whispered that a few times, he'd asked her a question or two himself.

From almost the day of his birth, his Gran had cooed in his ear that *he* was destined for great things, something she'd never said to his brother—and her words had proven true. How else could a poor lad from County Cork find himself on the brink of being named a director to the powerful East India Company?

But it wasn't just money his Gran had offered. "*When you meet this woman, hold on to her,*" she'd said. "*Your children's children will be dukes and princes. They will stride the world. But first, you must meet the woman.*"

"*Why will I need her?*" he'd asked. "*Mr. Fralin says I'm the smartest pupil he's ever taught. I don't need a lass to help me be important.*"

His Gran had cupped his chin with her cold, frail hand. "*You are right, my chava, but she will not be just any woman. She will be your destiny. Your purpose.*"

To a boy, such talk was gibberish. Like every other Irish lad his age, Fyclan was mad for horses and adventure. This talk of "purpose" had been beyond his understanding—especially when it involved lasses. He was going to be a military man. He would win honor and glory and own a stable of a fifty horses, and he wasn't going to share one of them with a lass.

However, now he was a man, and wiser to the ways of the world. He'd proven he understood money. He'd made fortunes for his superiors as well as a fortune for himself. There was no telling how far he could climb, especially since many whispered that Fyclan's smart leadership had saved the Company from another bankruptcy. It was commonly allowed that if he kept to his current path, he would someday be knighted.

And certainly, many of the current directors had their eye on him as a husband for their daughters, but Fyclan had not been tempted. No, he'd been waiting for *her*, the one his Gran had promised—the lady in blue with golden hair and creamy skin whose path had just crossed his.

Most gently bred young ladies of her age would be just finishing the morning toilettes after a night of balls and routs. Not this one. Crossing the street ahead of Fyclan, she walked with purpose. She glanced at her scrap of paper repeatedly, as if searching for an address. Her maid had to scamper to keep up with her. Her aggrieved footman held out his arm to protect her from the heavy traffic and unwarranted advances.

Fyclan crossed the street as well, wanting to keep her in his sights.

He didn't quite know how he would approach her or gain an introduction, but reach her he would—

His friend, Bishard, laid both hands on his arm and swung him around. He kept hold of Fyclan's jacket as he waved his hand in front of his face. "Are you not listening to me? Damn it all, Morris, I've never seen *you* chase a woman before, and now you charge off like a hound on the trace of a scent."

Fyclan laughed. "Only yesterday you chastised me for not being more aware of the fair sex. Well, now I am aware. Very aware. And I'm about to lose her, so excuse me—"

Bishard held fast. "*She's* not for you."

Those were fighting words. "And why not?"

His friend glanced around as if those on the pavement around them would be keenly interested in what he was about to say. His voice lowered. "Stowe has spoken for her."

He referred to the Marquess of Stowe, one of the wealthiest men in London. The directors of the Company were keenly interested in him. Not only did they want his money for investment, they also needed his political patronage.

Bishard's warning did give Fyclan pause. He looked in the direction of his goddess. She was moving steadily away, a bright blue gem weaving in and out amid a sea of drab, hardworking men and women, people whose lives held no room for such a lively color.

And he knew he must not lose her. "Who is Stowe to me?" he said, and would have charged off again in pursuit, but his friend held on.

"She is also Miss Jennifer Tarleton, *Colonel Russell Tarleton*'s daughter."

"The fool who cost us Konkan?" Fyclan referred to the battle the Company had fought against the Maratha rulers over the northern provinces. Fyclan had been the Company officer in charge and had removed Tarleton from his command. Fyclan had then been forced to lead the counteroffensive himself, barely saving the Company from a humiliating defeat. The scales had weighed in his favor that day but Fyclan had been well aware matters could have gone the opposite way.

"The same. And still just as foolish. From what I understand, he is in dun territory. His only hope is to marry his daughter to a trunkful of gold. Trust me, Morris, you don't want this one."

"I have money."

"But not as much as Stowe," Bishard answered.

Fyclan wasn't certain he was correct. However, before he could argue the point, Bishard continued, "There is bad blood between you and Tarleton. You cost the man his commission. You ruined him. He'd never sell his daughter to you. And you are aware how much power the marquess has? How crossing him might not be a wise choice?"

"Until a lass is married, she is fair game."

"True, unless there is a sizeable wager in the betting books of every club in this city that Stowe will win her hand. 'Tis said Stowe made the wager himself. He won't appreciate competition. You know they've charged Tillbury with bringing Stowe on board." Tillbury was the Company director to whom Fyclan and Bishard reported. "You have a lot to lose, my friend, if you earn Stowe's wrath."

The beauty in blue had stopped at a corner. Again, she checked her paper. Miss Tarleton had found the street she'd sought and in a blink would be completely out of Fyclan's sight.

Out of his life.

"Perhaps," he allowed to his friend. "Then again, some risks are worth the costs."

With that, Fyclan shook off Bishard's arm and began running to catch up.

Chapter Two

She needed a book. She had to have something to read. She was desperate for it.

Any book could be an escape. A good book, especially so. And books had saved Miss Jennifer Tarleton's sanity on occasions too numerous to count. A good hour of reading always eased her troubled mind and revived her spirits. A well-told tale put matters in perspective. This was how Jenny had coped with the challenges in her life, provided she could place her hands on something to read.

Her family didn't understand. They were not readers. Indeed, if it hadn't been for Jenny's sickly childhood and a kind and caring nurse, she would not have valued books as much as she did, either.

At home in Lansdown, Jenny borrowed books from her neighbors or Mr. Wheeler, the minister. Unfortunately, here in London, there was not one book to be had in the house her family had let for the season, and most of the people she'd met in London looked at her cross-eyed when she said she enjoyed reading. One young buck had even questioned, "Books? *You* read books?" He'd even shuddered as he spoke.,

However, after the angry scene she'd just witnessed between her parents, she was forced to take bold measures. At the gaming tables, her father continued to lose money that they just didn't have. When the amount of his debts were finally admitted, her mother had called for her smelling salts and taken to her room—in spite of her father's assurances that Jenny's future husband would save all.

Would her father ever learn? And why must it rest on Jenny's shoulders to marry a man wealthy enough to save him from debtor's prison? What if she failed? Her family would be ruined.

She was now grateful that she had learned the address of Sir David Littlefield, a renowned explorer and the owner of what was reputed to be one of the best libraries in the city. The other evening at the Barnhart rout, she'd overheard two gentlemen discussing their visit there. Apparently, Sir David opened his library to others.

She prayed he would allow her to borrow a book this afternoon. Just one book. Such a small request.

Jenny had been forced to sneak out of the house. Her father disliked her reading. "Reading will give you the squints, Jenny, and mar that lovely face of yours. Of course, marry the right man," he was fond of saying, "and you can have many books as you wish. But I'm not paying for them out of my pocket."

Marry the right man . . . there was the root of the problem.

Jenny had been born with the looks that men appreciated. Even when she was younger, doors that others found closed were opened for her. Favors were always pushed her way, while other lasses struggled to receive the simplest of courtesies. Since Jenny had matured into her looks, suitors had fought battles, both verbal and on rare occasion with fists, for her attention, but not one of them had captured her interest, let alone her heart.

Jenny had not asked for this trip to London. Fate was fickle. She of all people knew that. She had done nothing to earn the pleasing arrangement of her face. It was a gift from her Maker. Indeed, when men were too effusive about her looks, she found herself suspicious of their motives. They praised her, but they didn't know her. They weren't interested in her opinions or even in light banter. Her father had taken her aside several times over the past weeks, and said, "Just smile; don't yammer."

Only books didn't constantly weigh her value to them.

For a second, Jenny experienced one of her dizzy spells. She paused on the street, her footman, Lorry, hovering anxiously over her. "Do you need to return, Miss Jenny?"

She shook her head. "I will be fine." She hoped it was true. It had been over a year since she'd had one of her "spells." Usually, she paced herself, taking a bit of time every afternoon to rest. She had no desire to faint on such a crowded, busy street. She forced a smile and continued. She was so close to Sir David's address.

When she was born, her mother claimed Jenny's skin

was so blue, no one thought she would live a fortnight ... but she had. Granted, she'd had many spells when she was a child, but she had grown stronger with age. And while she sensed her days on this earth were carefully numbered, she was determined to live her life fully.

So, was it wrong to hope to meet a man like the ones she read about in novels? Adventurous men, daring men, empathetic and compassionate men? Men who were not like her father or most of the others she had met? She could envy her sister Serena's Evan, the squire's son ... but, *please God*, she would appreciate it if this imaginary man, born out of her reading and dreaming, was a great deal more intelligent than her sister's plodding beau.

And was it too much to ask that he be handsome, articulate, and somewhat younger than the Marquess of Stowe or any of the other gentlemen toward whom her father pushed her?

She and her servants reached Sir David's address. The neighborhood was eminently respectable. The façade of his house was marble and well tended.

"Lorry, stay here and wait on the step," Jenny instructed her footman. She knew he understood he must serve as lookout. He would warn her if he saw any signs of her father.

"Yes, Miss," Lorry answered, his glum tone pricking her conscience.

"I know I put you in a terrible position by threatening to leave without you. If I am caught, I will tell Father you had no choice."

"I'll still receive the sack."

That was true. "I shall return as quickly as possible. Come, Mandy."

The maid had accompanied her from Lansdown and was always intimidated to be out and about in London. She followed meekly as Jenny climbed the steps and lifted the knocker on the impressive black-lacquered door.

She didn't even have a moment to draw a breath when the door opened. The servant who answered was slender and tall. Very tall, and Jenny was a good height for a woman. He wore a turban around his head, and his features appeared to be cut from brown stone. "Yes, ma'am, may I help you?"

Jenny skewed her courage. London was different than Lansdown. People were not friendly. But she wanted a book.

"I would like to speak to Sir David."

"Sir David is away for the year."

"Oh." Her heart fell. Her anticipation had been high. She'd not considered what she'd do if her benefactor was not at home. "I see," she murmured, then, determined, said, "I wished to borrow a book from his library. I hear it is one of the finest in London."

"Are you a subscriber?"

"Subscriber?"

"Sir David's library is open to subscribers. If you wish to become a member—"

"A member?" She drew a breath and released it. Of course. How naïve of her. She'd heard of private lending libraries. "I should have realized," she said, speaking more to herself than the servant. Nor would she ask after the costs of the subscriptions. She had no money of her own. Not even pin money.

She was now glad Sir David was not at home. Indeed, she should remove herself from this doorstep with all haste before someone on the street recognized her—except she found it hard to move. Disappointment made her desperate.

"I *need* to borrow only one book," she said, as if hoping the servant could pull a tome from the pocket of his dark green livery and hand it to her. "I *must*."

"I'm sorry, Miss, the library is for subscribers only—"

"Childs," a deep male voice said from behind her, "let this gentlewoman use *my* subscription as my guest."

Jenny whirled in surprise. She could not accept such a gift from a strange man. She had been so caught up in her setback, she'd not even been aware of his approach.

However, once she turned, her polite protest died on her lips.

Standing on the stop below her was the most attractive man she had yet to meet. He was what a poet should look like—curling black hair, intelligent brown eyes dark with mystery, a lean jaw, and a wide and sensitive mouth.

There was a confidence about him, a certainty. He was looking at Jenny in the same manner she was taking him in, and he liked what he saw. She knew, because she was pleased as well. They were both obviously caught in the same spell.

The gentleman's standing with her was also boosted by Childs's eager change of attitude. "Hello, Mr. Morris. It is good to see you again, sir."

"Thank you, Childs." Mr. Morris's eyes did not leave Jenny. "You will accept my offer," he said to her. "It would give me great pleasure."

Jenny knew she shouldn't. However, lost in the dark amber depths of his eyes, she was having difficulty finding words to speak.

Childs saved her from trouble. "You know I can't do that, sir. Sir David doesn't approve of subscription holders loaning their privileges to others."

"Then I shall buy a subscription for this lady. Sir David will approve of that, no?"

"As you say, sir."

Jenny found her voice. She had no idea how much subscriptions cost, but any amount would be too much. She did not want Mr. Morris to form the wrong opinion of her. "I can't accept such a gift."

He raised his hand as if denying her claim. "I noticed you walking toward this house. No, I noticed you *marching* toward this house. You moved with great purpose, and I knew you would not be happy until you had achieved your goal. When I overheard you asking to see the library—well, few people surprise me, Miss—" He paused, waiting for her to fill in the introduction.

Jenny wasn't certain what was correct under these circumstances. Her mother had warned all of her daughters not to speak to strangers in London.

But she couldn't have meant Mr. Morris. Indeed, Jenny had the heady sensation that she knew him, that perhaps she had even been waiting for him to enter her life.

"Tarleton," she said, supplying the word he wanted.

"Tarleton," he repeated although she sensed he had already known her name.

"And you are?"

"Fyclan Morris," he answered. "And I, too, value reading." He smiled at her then, a smile that made her light-headed, and not in the dizzy, weak way of her spells. No, this was a very pleasant feeling. How criminal it was for so much charm to be tucked into one man's expression.

"You are Irish?" she asked because of his accent.

"Proudly so."

Well, he might be proud, but her father would not approve. He did not like the Irish. Nor would he ever approve of a mere "mister" when he believed Jenny could marry a marquess.

But then, Jenny was growing tired of her father's dictates, and what harm was there in smiling back?

Jenny offered him her gloved hand. "It is a pleasure to make your acquaintance, Mr. Morris."

He hesitated before taking her hand. If she hadn't been watching him so closely, she might have missed it. He acted as if he wanted to savor the moment.

How intriguing.

His fingers wrapped around hers. They were strong, long and lean in his gloves, and she wondered how his body would feel if he pulled her forward into his arms—?

From where had that thought come?

Mr. Morris had the devil's own smile and a presence that compelled her toward him. A wise woman would run, and Jenny had always been wise, always discreet.

Except when Mr. Morris released her hand, and said to Childs, "Well, man, are you going to leave us on the doorstep?" and the servant stepped aside, Jenny didn't back away.

Instead, when Mr. Morris approvingly indicated with a sweep of his hand for her to go ahead of him, she did.

After all, she wanted a book . . . didn't she?

Chapter Three

ASTUTE INTELLIGENCE AND a fantastic luck had carried Fyclan far in life—but *this* was different.

Miss Jennifer Tarleton was a treasure of the greatest value. She *read*! She valued *books*. Her physical beauty now blossomed in his mind when coupled with her intelligence.

Fyclan would not be the man he was today if he had not received access to Mr. Rodwell Neary's library when he was a boy. Books had taken a lad of common parentage and given him uncommon opportunities in life. Through the adventure of reading, Fyclan had dared to dream. He particularly enjoyed history and biographies of great men.

And now, he was facing the dream of any man's lifetime. He was in the presence of his destiny. Over the years, he'd met many women, but he'd waited for *the one*. He'd believed she'd existed for no other reason than his

Gran's assurance, and now, Miss Tarleton was his reward for his patient trust.

Sir David's front hall was the size of a ballroom. The house had been in the family since the Restoration. The floor was of uneven squares of gray marble, and the wood paneling was covered with a variety of exotic spears, sabers, and the horns and skins of dead animals.

"Oh dear," Miss Tarleton whispered.

Fyclan nodded with understanding. "I'm here often enough I've become accustomed to it. Sir David is proud of his collection."

"Yes," she said in a subdued voice.

"I, on the other hand, find it a bit much," he confided. "However, his library is worth the extravagance. This way. Subscribers are allowed the freedom of the house to search out the library on their own. Sir David is rarely at home, and he takes pleasure in sharing his books."

At the mention of the library, Miss Tarleton's eyes lit up. "I heard it is hard to imagine."

"One of the best collections in the world and a fitting location for it," Fyclan acknowledged.

"Wait here for me, Mandy," she said to her maid, indicating a chair by the front door. She then followed Fyclan down the narrow hall to wooden double doors. The latch appeared ancient and was probably a trinket Sir David had picked up during his travels. Fyclan opened the doors, first one, then the other, so that Miss Tarleton could have the full effect of the library.

Her reaction was all he had anticipated and mimicked his own when he had first walked into this room.

"I've *never* see the *like*," she breathed in admiration. She moved into the room, with its line of fully stocked bookcases, one after another, from one wall to the next.

Desks were available for study, complete with ornate oil lamps. Comfortable chairs formed a gathering place in the middle of the room beneath a domed ceiling.

Miss Tarleton moved to the center of the room and looked up at the paintings gracing the dome. They were of Athena, the goddess of Wisdom, and her minions. They rode in chariots or lounged on clouds.

"This is amazing." She glanced around the room. "We are the only ones here in this wealth of knowledge."

"Sir David is particular about whom he allows into his sanctuary," Fyclan answered. Childs had come in behind them. He now took a stance at the desk nearest the door, assuming his duties as keeper of the library.

"I can understand why." She moved toward the books, placing a reverent hand on the leather-covered spines. She glanced at him, her eyes sparkling with the pleasure of a book lover. "This speaks *well* for your credibility, Mr. Morris."

"Which has been my intention all along, Miss Tarleton."

She laughed, the sound so light Fyclan could imagine it being the music of angels. She disappeared among the bookcases. "I don't know where to begin," she called. "Sir David can't have read all of these?"

"These books have been in his family for generations." Fyclan moved toward the sound of her voice.

"I would never leave the house with all this to read," she declared. "I would be in heaven."

That was the same reaction Fyclan had experienced when he'd first visited the library. "Sir David is not particular about how many books one borrows. The rule is if you do not return a volume, your subscription will be abruptly ended. Childs marks every book that leaves this room."

"Is that true, Childs?" Miss Tarleton called, her voice coming from the far corner of the library.

"Mr. Morris is very correct."

Miss Tarleton's lovely head popped out from behind a bookcase. "I don't know where to begin," she whispered in wonder. "There is so much here." She stepped from behind the bookcase. "Thank you, Mr. Morris, thank for this generous gift. I should not accept it from you, and yet, I am powerless to refuse. You may have saved my sanity."

If Fyclan had slain a dragon for her, he could not have been more proud.

He had won his lady's interest. The cost of the subscription was a mere pittance to him; however, the smile she gave him was worth more than gold.

"Start anywhere," he managed to say. Her smile had the power to unman him or throw him into unrivaled lust.

She took his advice and started perusing the section closest at hand. "Maps," she whispered. "This is a shelf of maps. No, wait. This whole case is *shelves* of maps." She shook her head as if bemused by the extravagance and moved on.

"Biographies," she announced, delighted. She pulled a

book from the shelf and did something he always did—she opened the cover, flipped a few pages, and breathed deep.

She caught his eye and smiled as if abashed. "I like the smell of paper."

"I do as well," he said, walking toward her.

Her dark lashes swept down as she turned her attention to the book. "Sometimes I imagine even the letters have their own scent. These are bold and black, like a strong tea." She reached for another book and opened it. "These are old, and the ink is fading. They remind me of my grandmother. She was so brittle with age, yet she was still a force to be reckoned with. We all did exactly as she expected."

"You must read a great deal of the poets," Fyclan said.

Color rose to her cheeks. "I do go on. My family teases me when they think I am silly, especially when I start quoting philosophers. 'The opinions of dead men,' is what my father says." She'd gruffed up her voice to ape her sire, an amusing bit, but the smile left her face as quickly as it had come, almost as if the thought of her father troubled her.

He took the book from her. "Reading is not always valued," he murmured. "It takes discipline. Concentration. Intelligence." He shelved the book of grandmotherly letters, and added, "I admire your ability to enjoy the very moment of life, to see pleasure in the small things."

His compliment was sincere, and he had hoped to please her.

Instead, a sadness came to her eyes. It was there in the depths.

"I meant no insult, Miss Tarleton."

His apology startled her. "I took no insult, sir. Indeed I'm—" She stopped as if reconsidering her words. Her brows came together. "I must not tarry. I've already taken much of your time."

He could have told her she could have *all* his time, every golden minute of it. He wanted to keep her forever.

Her gaze fell on a book sitting halfway out on a lower shelf. She leaned and pulled it out. She opened to the title page, and said with some surprise, "Sir David wrote this book. It is a journal."

Fyclan remembered reading it. "Is it the tale of his time in Ceylon?"

She smiled, without the shadows in her eyes. "*Ceylon Sojourn*," she agreed. "His *personal* journal. Do you believe he'd let me borrow it?"

"Of course he will. He let me do so. This collection is to share. If you like reading about exotic places, you will enjoy it. Sir David is an excellent writer although he can be a bit salty."

"Salty?"

"He's a blunt man and enjoys sharing his experiences. *All* of them. Some of them are very dramatic."

She laughed her happiness. "I enjoy drama, when it is in books." She wrapped her arms around the journal. "Then this is the one I would like to borrow. My father was once in Ceylon."

"Then Colonel Tarleton should approve." The words came out of his mouth because *he* approved, and he was ridiculously happy over the book she'd chosen. He'd watched as she'd lingered over the biographies and maps. She hadn't even looked at the volumes of fiction. He himself enjoyed a piece of literature now and then. Stories could be fascinating, but the world was a big place, as Fyclan knew firsthand, and he often thought real tales more interesting. Her intellectual curiosity only added to her allure.

Yes, *she was the one*.

"You know that my father was in the military?" she asked, having caught his slip, revealing knowledge of her sire.

"Of course I've heard of the valiant Colonel Tarleton." At another time, Fyclan would have choked on the words in speaking them. He wondered what she thought of the colonel. Did she worship him as a hero? Could he stomach such a thought?

If he wooed and won Miss Tarleton, the colonel would be related to him by marriage. There was a thought to give a man pause—

Suddenly, the library clock chimed . . .

"Oh dear, the time is passing. I *must* leave," she said. "I'm terribly sorry to be so abrupt. I am supposed to attend a musicale this evening. Thank you, again, Mr. Morris. Thank you." She had already started moving to the door as she spoke, holding the book out to Childs to record. She sounded rattled, as if Fyclan's mention of her father had reminded her of where she was, what she was doing.

He wanted to stop her from leaving. He wanted her to stay here with him until he knew her every secret, want, and desire—which would take a lifetime.

Instead, he came to stand by her side. The scent of her

pleased him. She smelled of field flowers as they warmed in the summer sun . . . apparently she brought out the poet in him as well.

"I shall read Sir David's book and return it forthright," she promised Fyclan, taking the book from Childs.

And then she did the most amazing thing. She touched Fyclan. Her gloved fingers lightly brushed his arm, the barest hint of a caress, but it sparked a hunger in him. He wanted more.

Instinctively, he reached for her, but she'd already moved away, her arms around her book. She was out the double doors in a blink and moving rapidly down the hall.

"Come, Mandy," she called. Her maid fell into step behind her. Childs raced to reach the front door and open it for her.

Fyclan rushed forward as if to stop her, but Miss Tarleton did not linger on the front step. By the time he reached the door, she was moving with her customary purpose toward the busy main thoroughfare, rushing as if to an appointment and fearing she would be late.

For a little more than a quarter of an hour, he had basked in the presence of his destiny, and now she was walking away.

But then, at the corner, she stopped and looked back. Her gaze found his. She raised a hand and gave him a small wave before disappearing from his view.

Yes, she had looked for him.

He struggled with the urge to chase after her. Then again, half the men in London probably shared that same struggle.

But she was *his*. He knew it all the way to his bones. She would be the mother of his children. *You chose well, Gran.*

"She is stunning, isn't she, sir?" Childs remarked.

Fyclan was not surprised that Jennifer Tarleton had made an impact on even the taciturn manservant. She had completely changed *his* life.

"More than stunning," Fyclan answered. He pulled a guinea from his pocket. "When she returns the book, send someone for me. My offices are around the corner. You know where."

Childs palmed the coin. "I will do so, sir."

But that wasn't going to be enough for Fyclan. No, if an Irish mongrel like him wanted to win the heart of a woman with such sparkling intelligence, he needed to be more clever than her other suitors. And he could not be shy.

Then he remembered what Bishard had said. The betting books across the city were weighted heavily in favor of Stowe, the man his superiors in the Company were seeking as an investor.

Stowe was a pompous fool. He also had a gut the size of a whale. A man like him should not consider himself worthy of a jewel like Miss Tarleton although he had no doubt Stowe and the colonel meshed together very well.

If it was money Tarleton wanted for his daughter, Fyclan had plenty of it and would receive even more when he was named director. However, if it was a title and prestige, well, Fyclan could be out of the running.

Then there was the problem that he and Tarleton were the bitterest of enemies.

"This one is up to you, Gran," he said under his breath. "If she's meant for me, then I'll need your help." With those words, he walked to the Company's offices. It was not unusual for him to ask for his gypsy grandmother's help. There had been many a time when Fyclan had been in a tight spot and sent her a prayer. She always delivered.

And today was no different.

Bishard was waiting for Fyclan at his desk. "Where the bloody hell have you been? The Old Cracker has been asking for you. I have assured him you were out on business—"

"*Mr. Morris*, it is about time you honored us with your presence," Mr. Charles Tillbury, also known as the Old Cracker, as in whip, said from the door of his office. "Come here."

When the Old Cracker used his senatorial tone, one didn't know what to expect. Fyclan exchanged a wary glance with Bishard before approaching his superior.

"Yes, sir?"

Tillbury had a military bearing although he also enjoyed the soft life. He wore a dark brown bag wig that was at odds with the lines of age on his face. "The Marquess of Stowe has finally condescended to read the proposal you prepared about the Sumatra voyage."

"That was six months ago."

"He now says he is interested."

"But you have doubts?"

"No one can afford doubts with a man whose purse is as fat as Stowe's. I want to tap his pocket, Mr. Morris. If not Sumatra, then something else. He needs a nudge, but he says he doesn't have time for a meeting to discuss the matter."

"What are you proposing?"

"That we take our interests to him. Dangle them in front of him like bait. He will be at Lord and Lady Nestor's musicale this evening. You remember Lord Nestor?"

"I do. You went to school with him."

"Aye, and he has given me invitations for this evening. Put on your dancing shoes, Mr. Morris, we are going out in society. But you'd best be sharp. We've wanted Stowe's backing for a long time. This is your chance to bring him in for us."

"Mine alone?"

"What do I know of Sumatra? However, do this, and you will have earned you director's seat. The youngest man ever elected. Go on with you. Be ready. This might be the most important night of your life."

He was right.

Jennifer Tarleton was attending a musicale that evening. She had told him so in the library.

"I appreciate the opportunity, sir," Fyclan said, meaning those words.

"See that you make the most of it," Mr. Tillbury advised.

"Oh, I shall."

Chapter Four

MR. MORRIS HAD been watching her leave.

Elation brought heat to Jenny's cheeks as she ducked her head, turned the corner, and jigged in triumph right there in the street.

Scurrying behind her, Mandy almost collided with her. "Oh, sorry, Miss."

"Don't be sorry, be *happy*," Jenny answered generously, wanting to share her good mood. "Come, Lorry, let's hurry before my absence is noticed."

"That is what I've been trying to do, Miss Jenny," the sometime surly footman muttered, and she just laughed, clutching her book to her chest as the footman used his big body to shield her from gawkers and the rude along the busy street. Mandy had to skip a step to keep up with them.

Fyclan Morris. What a strange and brash name. Fyclan. She'd never met an Irishman before. Her father would not have approved.

And yet, Fyclan Morris was everything she had hoped to meet in a gentleman and hadn't yet. For the first time in her life, she felt as if she could fall in love.

Love, yes, just like the poets praised, and Mr. Morris was certainly poem worthy. He was handsome. She liked his strong nose, his almost black eyes, his square jaw.

She liked even more that he had spoken *to* her. Not *about* her. Not *around* her. Not *through* her.

To her.

And he had behaved as if he didn't find her bookish tendencies disagreeable. Her mother constantly warned her to not talk about books or art or music. *Listen, Jenny, listen. Use your ears more than your mouth. That is what men appreciate in a woman.*

There was great truth in her mother's advice. Jenny had noted the quieter she was, the more the gentleman did like her, mainly because they had more room to talk about themselves. They liked looking at her but didn't act as if they wished to know her.

However, Fyclan Morris had asked questions as if her answers interested him. He hadn't patronized her when she chose Sir David's book. He'd actually encouraged her to read the text in spite of its being salty—*oh, she couldn't wait to discover exactly what he meant.*

He was also the first man of her acquaintance in London not to comment about her height. It was true she wasn't petite, but she wasn't taller than her sisters. Her mother, too, had a good height. Still, gentlemen in London seemed to find her five-foot-ten unusual, especially those men who were shorter than she.

Mr. Morris might have been a half inch or an inch shorter, and yet, she didn't believe he'd found her freakish at all.

No, when he looked at her, she felt admired . . . and she could return the appreciation. He was perfectly made, a prime specimen of a gentleman.

"Here we are, Miss Jenny," Lorry said, directing her down the back alley behind a row of houses. "Hurry now. It is half past one. You may have callers waiting."

Jenny doubted it. Her observation was that gentlemen of the noble class did not venture out until three. There might be flowers, but no callers.

She understood Lorry's concern. Of the three of them, his absence might be the most noticed since he served as butler when they had callers and as her father's valet when needed. All of the other Tarleton servants were female. Their wages were lower, and there was no tax charged on female help.

Jenny set aside thoughts of Mr. Fyclan Morris. She had more important matters to consider, such as sneaking into her house with her precious book. She held her breath as they entered the gate leading to the tiny garden. She dashed across the grass, praying no one saw her, and hurried up the house's back step.

Mandy went in first. Lorry and Jenny waited, until Mandy said, "It is fine to enter."

Lorry held the door open for Jenny to rush inside. She breathed easier once she was under her roof. There could now be few questions asked that she couldn't answer.

"We'd best not test our luck again, Miss," Lorry informed her. "We made it once, but we were lucky."

Jenny didn't answer. Both servants were devoted to her, and she knew when she asked him to do so, Lorry would help her at any time

And she would ask him. She had to return the book and perhaps see Mr. Morris again.

Lorry's expression said he knew what she was thinking. He went off with a grumble to fulfill his other duties around the house.

Mandy took Jenny's hat. "Are you wearing the cream dress this evening to the musicale?"

"Yes, and with the blue overdress," Jenny answered. She preferred simple styles and had managed to wear this cream-colored cotton dress a number of ways by changing the sashes and using overdresses that she and her sisters had stitched themselves. When one's father gambled the way hers did, one had to economize. "I will be right up."

"Yes, Miss," Mandy said before taking the servants' stairs to the floor where the family slept.

Carrying her precious book, Jenny walked toward the staircase at the front of the house, the one the family was expected to use. As she approached the sitting room, she heard copious weeping.

The door was closed. She knew before opening it that Serena was the one crying.

Her sister sat on the settee, hunched over as tears flowed. A sympathetic Alice had an arm around her. Her sisters were respectively three and fours years older than she. Consequently, Serena and Alice were very close. This was also their first trip to London, and they had made it clear to Jenny they were very conscious of the fact that only because of her were they here. Worse, they had to share a bedroom because the colonel decreed that Jenny deserved privacy since this trip was all about her success on the marriage market. It would be Jenny who needed the rest after spending her evenings at balls and parties. It was Jenny who got the lovely gowns. And it was Jenny who needed to secure their futures.

Jealousy was an ugly emotion, and over the past four weeks that they'd been in the city, Jenny had felt the sting of her sisters' too many times for comfort. They were both lovely women . . . but Jenny was the one lauded as the "beauty."

Seeing the unwelcoming expression on her sisters' faces, Jenny had an uneasy feeling that she would regret opening the door.

"Is something the matter?" she asked.

"Serena's heart has been broken," Alice answered.

Jenny set aside the book and rushed to kneel on the floor beside Serena. "What happened?"

"The Squire Paulson is refusing to let Evan and me marry," Serena choked out before breaking down in sobs again.

Alice spoke for her. "Evan was here an hour ago with the news. She has been like this ever since."

"Where is Mother?" Jenny asked.

"Still in bed with smelling salts. I told her Evan decamped and why. She is furious with the Paulsons."

Serena raised her head. "They wish Evan to marry his cousin, Rebecca. Her family has property they want, but,

Jenny, if you marry someone important, then they will relent. They will let me marry Evan. I *know* they will."

Jenny rocked back. "Isn't that shallow of them?" she dared to say.

"Shallow to expect you to be responsible to your family?" Alice snapped. "Be practical, Jenny. You have an opportunity to do something the rest of us can't. You must rescue the family from father's vices. He'd promised Wills that he would help him secure an advancement last year, and still nothing has happened." Wills was her husband of two years. He was a lieutenant in the infantry and eager for promotion, a promotion that he would buy.

"I'm here in London," Jenny pointed out. "No one has offered. I'm doing what I can. Or would you prefer we set up an auction block on the front step and send me off with the highest bidder?"

"So dramatic," Alice answered. "Apparently we have an actress in the family."

"Your patience is impressive," Jenny coolly shot back.

"*I'm* tired of being patient," Serena said. "I'm tired of waiting. I am growing old and gray, and no one cares. All Mother and Father think about is *Jenny* and being certain *Jenny* has what will make the right impression. No one ever thinks about me."

"Or Wills and me," Alice agreed.

"At least you have Wills," Serena threw in.

Jenny had heard this complaint from her sisters before. They resented everything done for Jenny that was also not done for them—and Jenny understood. She would be frustrated as well.

She also hated the pressure of being the one expected to sacrifice for the family.

"Do you believe Evan still has feelings for you?" she asked Serena.

"I know he does. He was downhearted when he delivered the news. His hands were shaking."

"Then why doesn't he defy his parents and fight for his love?"

Alice reached over and picked up the book. "Are you reading Shakespeare again?"

Jenny grabbed the borrowed book back from her. "No, but I will tell you that if this was one of Shakespeare's plays, Evan wouldn't make excuses for his parents. He would sweep Serena into his arms and elope."

Both sisters stared at her as if she had taken leave of her senses.

Alice spoke first. "Or, Serena, you and Evan can act out the last scene of *Romeo and Juliette* and drink poison or stab yourselves to death."

"Or we could have asps bite us like the ending of *Antony and Cleopatra*," Serena suggested bitterly.

Jenny made an impatient sound and rose to her feet, holding Sir David's book close as she did. "Fine. What do I know?" She started for the door but then whirled around. "If Evan were worthy of you, he'd stand up to his parents for you." She believed this with all her heart.

Serena jumped to her feet, her color high. "Listen to you—someone who has *never* been in love. But what do you care? *You* won't have children. The good doctor. Higley warns us that childbirth could kill you. Does it matter whom you marry? Mr. Higley even told Mother you could die at any moment anyway."

The words were ugly.

For a second, they hovered in the air between the sisters, then Serena's face crumpled. "I didn't mean that to sound so cruel, Jenny," she said.

Jenny held up a hand to stave her off, stunned by Serena's words. "You only spoke the truth."

"Jenny, please, Serena didn't mean—" Alice started, but Jenny interrupted her.

"*I know* what she meant." Jenny released her breath. She wanted to pretend it didn't matter. It did.

Jenny looked down at the book she held. "You married for love, Alice. You want to marry for love, Serena. Why is it you believe I should marry to settle Father's finances? Is it because my health makes me dispensable?" she asked, as they remained silent. "Are you just being practical?"

She turned, planning to leave the room with her head high. Let her sisters stew in their own consciences.

However, before she could make her exit, the door flew open, and her father came striding into the room, his hat set forward on his wig at a cocky angle. He took her by both arms and swung her around. "*Jenny*, my girl, have I news."

He was a tall man with a strong nose and booming voice that had once commanded men. He still wore his uniform although he was fully retired.

"I want you to look lively tonight," he said. "Stowe is about to come up to scratch. He's been asking questions about how much I'd be willing to take for your hand.

And"—he paused for effect, his blue eyes aglow with excitement—"they *say* he made a *wager* in the betting book at Brooks's that one Miss Jennifer Tarleton would soon become a *marchioness*." He ended his statement with a triumphant clap of his hand, then looked around expectantly, as if believing she should be excited as well.

And he was disappointed.

"What?" he asked. "Are you not happy, Jenny? What of you other girls? Did you hear what I said? Stowe will come up to scratch."

In response, Serena burst into tears all over again and collapsed upon the settee.

Alice spoke for them. "Yes, we are happy." She did not even glance at Jenny. Perhaps after the scene a moment ago, she was too embarrassed.

Their father turned to Jenny. "And what of you? You did it, girl. *You did it.* We are in the money now."

As he crowed, the image of Mr. Fyclan Morris's handsome face rose in her mind, and the image turned to dust. Her stomach twisted painfully.

"Jenny?" her father said. "Are you all right?"

"Yes, fine," she managed to say, unnerved by how upset she was to hear Stowe would make an offer. Hours ago, she would have been relieved. After all, this is why they'd come to London—

"What is that you are carrying?" the colonel said, obviously annoyed that his news was not being met by rejoicing. "A book? Another book, Jenny? No wonder you are upset. Reading isn't good for a woman's mind. Let me have that."

Before she realized what he was about, he snatched the book out of her hands. He flipped the pages, holding it out of her reach.

"I *borrowed* that book, Father," she said. "It isn't mine. I need to take care of it."

"Where did you find it?"

"I told you I borrowed it."

"From whom?"

Jenny thought fast. "Mrs. Rockwell, our neighbor."

He hummed his thoughts. "Mrs. Rockwell is reading about Ceylon? Interesting." He closed the book.

"May I have it back?"

A cunning look stole over his face, a look that never boded well for Jenny. "Why, yes, daughter, you may . . . once you have landed the Marquess of Stowe. I don't want anything to distract you until you have taken care of your family. Right, girls?"

Her sisters didn't respond, but their silence didn't bother the colonel. He waved the precious book at Jenny before charging up the front-hall stairs, a self-satisfied whistle on his lips.

Chapter Five

JENNY HAD NEVER been so angry in her life.

That book was not her father's to do with as he wished. She had an obligation to Mr. Morris to see it safely returned to Sir David's library.

She also knew the pitfalls of raising a fuss. Her father would ask questions. He could be capricious. If he discovered she'd sneaked out of the house to go to Sir David's library, he might shrug, *or* he might interpret her actions as an affront to his authority. He could even take out his displeasure on Lorry and Mandy, and Jenny definitely didn't wish that to happen.

The truth was, she didn't know her father well. He'd been gone most of her life. Military duties had taken him to foreign shores. He'd made only rare appearances until he'd retired from military service.

She decided her best choice was to bide her time.

Consequently, on the coach ride to Lord and Lady

Nestor's musicale, she was quiet. Her sisters, too, were silent. Serena had dried her tears, but her air was melancholy. Alice refused to look at Jenny.

In contrast, their parents were giddy with excitement. The colonel was absolutely convinced that Stowe would speak to him tonight . . . or to Jenny. "If he steps out of the lines of traditional propriety, let him! A man with nothing but daughters can't be too choosy when someone is willing to take one of them off his hands."

He laughed at his own small jest. Jenny forced a smile. The colonel had used this statement more than once. His words reminded Jenny of family stories about how disappointed he'd grown with each daughter born.

Her mother, a thin, quiet woman who had shepherded her daughters over the years when her husband had been away, held Jenny's hand in a tight squeeze. Her blue eyes, the ones so much like Jenny's, shone with anticipation.

Jenny understood. Her father's fortunes had been precarious. There had been many times growing up when her mother had fretted over where to find the money to pay rent or the servants their wages. A marriage to Stowe would change all of that. He'd provide them with an income, one, Jenny cynically thought, the colonel would probably gamble away.

Still, she understood her responsibilities, and if she didn't, her family would happily clarify them for her. So, it was in a stoic frame of mind that she entered the large hall in Lord and Lady Nestor's house, where the musicale would take place. A pianoforte and several string instruments were set up in corner of the room in front of rows of gilded chairs

Lady Nestor prided herself in being a patroness of musicians in London. The singer tonight was a German fellow, well proportioned and blandly handsome with a huge voice. He was a particular favorite of the king's. Consequently, the room was crowded with those hoping His Majesty might make an appearance, something, Lady Nestor happily trilled to all around her, that *could* happen.

One of the bits of society that fascinated Jenny was how a rout or a ball was never exactly that. They were actually opportunities for the important to gather and discuss matters of mutual interest. 'Twas whispered that more acts and laws under consideration before Parliament were settled on the dance floors of London than in the corridors of the esteemed houses themselves.

Perhaps that is one of the reasons she did enjoy these social gatherings. She did not want to linger with the ladies and discuss milliners and compare seamstresses. Important topics fascinated Jenny. She enjoyed the comments she overheard from the powerful and seeing the outcomes reported a few days or even weeks later in the papers. Here was a glimpse into a world she had never imagined, and she found it intriguing.

As she followed her father and mother around the main room, she thought that one advantage to marrying Stowe is that she would stay in London. Another advantage was that, once married, no one would care who she was. Right now, she was given great accord because the gentlemen fancied her, but all the ogling would blessedly change—

Her father pulled up short. His body stiffened, and he hissed through his teeth.

"What is it, Colonel?" her mother asked.

"Fyclan Morris. Damn his hide. What is he doing here, talking to Stowe?"

"Fyclan Morris?" her mother echoed.

At the mention of the name, Jenny pushed forward, anxious to catch a glimpse of the man who had captured her interest that afternoon. *He was here.* And he looked even better in evening dress.

He wore his hair pulled back and unpowdered. His midnight-blue jacket seemed molded to his broad shoulders. His white knee breeches with silver buckles emphasized his lean masculinity. His shirt was a snowy white under a silver-gray vest. The knot in his neckcloth was impeccable.

In contrast, Lord Stowe appeared a rooster in his sea-green jacket and neckcloth of overflowing lace. He preferred a wig that added height to his frame, but Jenny thought its shape reminded her of nothing less than a coxcomb.

Her father yanked her back behind him. "Don't let Morris see Jenny," he ordered his family. "The man is bent on ruining me."

Ruin? A thousand questions leaped to Jenny's mind.

"Who is he?" her mother asked.

"A bastard through and through and an unmitigated liar. I knew him in India. Come, let us go as far away from him as possible."

"But Lord Stowe—" her mother started to protest.

"Will find Jenny," the colonel finished. He had taken Jenny's arm and directed her away from Mr. Morris—but she glanced back.

He was looking at her. He pretended to listen to Lord Stowe, but his gaze was on her, and she *knew* that he was here for her. She knew it.

She wanted to wave. More than that, she had the urge to run to him, to throw herself in his arms and tell him about what had happened to Sir David's book. But she didn't. Instead, she let her father lead her away to the room set aside for refreshments.

Nor would her father say anything else about Fyclan Morris in answer to the questions her mother did try to ask. Jenny was silent on the matter. Several gentlemen admirers gathered around her so that she could hide her interest in this enemy of her father's behind light teasing and easy banter, but she knew the moment Mr. Morris entered the refreshment room.

He stood in a corner talking to several gentlemen, yet he was aware of her. Just as aware as she was of him.

Stowe approached. He reminded her of nothing less than a huge, burly ram, one foot placed in front of the other and his head heavy from his own consequence. He brushed aside her younger admirers and bowed over her hand. "You appear radiant this evening, Miss Morris, as always."

"Thank you, my lord," she murmured, as her parents beamed their approval.

Stowe looked to the colonel and her mother. "You will allow me the honor of escorting your lovely daughter into the music room?"

"Of course, of course," her father said. "She was hoping you would ask."

Stowe offered Jenny his arm, and she felt she had no other option than to take it, conscious that Mr. Morris was a witness to it all.

They joined the flow of people moving into the music room. Her parents were behind them, then they seemed to melt back into the crowd. Lord Stowe escorted her to seats in the first rows. He preened and glanced around as if to see if everyone noticed him. Of course, they did. There was a bet on the books at Brooks's to ensure they would.

However, she had a disquieting sense that Lord Stowe wasn't interested in her at all. Not truly. He didn't bother to make small talk. Instead, he led her to his seats in the section reserved for the Very Important as if she were a mute prize.

While the musicians were warming up, she dared to lean toward His Lordship. "I saw you speaking to Mr. Morris earlier."

"You know him?" Stowe did not sound surprised.

"He recommended a book to me. How do you know him?"

"The East India Company wants me to invest in a venture Morris oversees. They say he can turn lead into gold, but I have my doubts. After all, he's Irish."

"Is that your *only* objection?" Jenny dared to ask.

Lord Stowe's gaze drifted over her, from her lips down to bodice, where he lingered. He smiled, the expression smugly complacent, as if he knew something no one else did.

"Morris is successful," he said, "but why are we talking about some grubby money manager? Especially when I find myself fortunate enough to be sitting beside London's current beauty. I'd rather talk about you."

Heat warmed her cheeks over the supposed compliment. Still, it didn't ring right in her ears. Instead, she was embarrassed by it. Nor was she surprised when a gentleman in the row of chairs in front of them leaned back to say something to Lord Stowe, and the marquess immediately forgot her. She was a bauble. A plaything. He wanted to be seen with her, but he wasn't attentive of her.

Was he trying to make other men jealous? Or, since as her father's daughter she'd learned a bit about the vagaries of gambling, was he interested in upsetting the betting book at Brooks's? What would he gain from such an endeavor?

With startling insight, Jenny knew right then that Stowe had *no* intention of offering for her. He just enjoyed showing her off. After all, the man was wealthy. What was the cost of a bet for his vanity?

Jenny abhorred the hypocrisy. Is this what her father desired for her? To be treated as if she had no value?

Without even thinking, she stood.

Heads turned. The German singer had opened his mouth to release the first note. He now shut it, as if affronted that she had moved. His accompanists stopped, and Lord Stowe gaped up at her.

Jenny pressed her hand to abdomen as if she had taken ill. "Excuse me, my lord, I need a moment of privacy." She didn't wait for permission but shuffled past the line of people sitting beside her. She reached the aisle and hurried with as much dignity as she could muster for the door.

Her mother caught up with her in the hall. "What is the matter?"

"Where is Father?"

Her mother's expression grew rueful. "He has disappeared into the gaming room. He said he doesn't wish to listen to foreign caterwauling."

The gaming room. Of course. There was one at every ball, every rout, every affair. He was probably gambling on the prospect of her marrying Stowe, and Jenny wondered if there would ever be an end it?

She took her mother by the arms. "You must stop him. You must pull him away before he loses more money."

"My dear, you know I can't do that to the colonel—"

Jenny gave her mother a shake. "Stowe is not going to offer for me. I sat next to the man. He wanted me there, but he barely even looked at me."

"Well, husbands can be that way—" her mother started, but Jenny wasn't hearing it.

"That is *not* the husband I want, Mother."

Jenny didn't know who was more astounded by her words—her mother, or herself. But the truth of her stand resonated in every fiber of her being.

"You must take him," her mother soberly. "Do you truly believe that I don't want what is best for you? You can escape this treacherous channel I've navigated all my life. If I had been wiser, if I'd had more direction from my parents, I would have married better, and that is my hope for you."

Jenny heard the love in her voice, the regret, and she wanted to scream. To rebel.

Her mother continued "Stowe and his sort may be boors, but they can afford to take proper care of you."

"And Father's debts?"

"No, I am talking about your life. What? Do you believe Mr. Higley is as knowledgeable as London doctors? You'd be wrong. Do you believe I don't notice those times when you are fatigued? You seem strong now, but there are moments you are very pale. If you marry well, you can have the very best of care. The most comfortable life. To be blunt: A fat purse might save you, Jenny. And we do not have that kind of money."

"But what value is there to life if I find myself strapped to a man who barely acknowledges me as little more than a possession? My life may be short, Mother, but I want it to count."

Her mother's lips parted as if she would protest, but then she closed them. She placed her hand against the side of Jenny's cheek, a tender gesture, then she stepped back. "I will see if I can remove your father from the gaming room. However, you must stay until the end of this evening so as not to give insult to Lord Stowe. You understand?"

"I understand. Thank you, Mother."

Her mother left the hall.

Jenny knew she should return to the musicale. Instead, she moved along to the hall to a door leading out into the garden. The fresh night air felt good on her heated skin. It felt honest, something she didn't feel inside.

If he'd been here, the good doctor Higley would have reprimanded her about the dangers of an excess of emotion. He'd always been warning her.

But she didn't care. In fact, it had felt good to act on her impulses. Good to speak her mind to her mother. The days when her skin was tinged were long behind her, and the last thing she wanted to think about was death.

Her hosts had not planned on anyone's visiting the garden. There were no lights other than from the windows. Otherwise, there was just blessed darkness and peace.

The door opened.

She could see a man's silhouette as he stepped out in the garden. He shut the door behind him. She recognized him immediately.

"My father wants me to marry for money, Mr. Morris."

"I have money," he answered.

"Yes," she agreed sadly. "But he considers you an enemy."

"I know."

And then she ran to him.

Chapter Six

SHE WAS COMING to him.

Fyclan opened his arms, unbelieving at his good luck.

He had not been able to take his eyes off Jennifer Tarleton from the moment she had stepped into Lord and Lady Nestor's house. She was grace personified even though he had sensed an air of turmoil around her.

Yes, he was *that* attuned to her spirit.

Tillbury had expected him to impress the Marquess of Stowe and assure him that Stowe's money could be placed in Fyclan's trust. Fyclan didn't give a damn for Stowe or his money. He'd come here to see her. He wanted to believe the connection he felt for her was mutual, and now here was proof.

And then, right before she could step into his arms, she pulled up short. She stood poised, as alert and fragile as a newborn foal trying to make sense of the world. She held her hands up, palms facing him. "Mustn't."

Such an ugly word.

"You can trust me," he answered, his voice barely a whisper lest he startle her and she run off.

"This is madness," she replied, half to herself.

"It is, but it is a good madness. In fact, it is the sort of madness that makes the world seem right."

She shifted her weight back. "Did you know who my father was when I met you today?"

He was tempted to lie. He didn't. "Yes."

"Do you wish to destroy him?"

"No."

"But you understand he is set against you."

"Yes."

Miss Tarleton took a moment to digest this. He could feel her doubts. Trust was a fragile, and valuable, commodity.

He knew.

Fyclan also knew he could not let her go.

"Father has taken Sir David's book from me."

Here was an acceptance, an opening, and yet he understood he must treat this small gift with the respect it deserved. "Does he know of our meeting today?"

"No. I lied about where I'd borrowed the book. I told him a neighbor woman lent it to me. I only learned of his dislike of you when he saw you talking to Lord Stowe." There was a beat of silence, then she said, "Father says he'll return the book once I accept His Lordship's marriage offer." Her gaze slid to a point on the ground only she could see as she admitted "Lord Stowe is not going to offer marriage. That is not his game. I realized that tonight."

Fyclan nodded. After a few minutes of listening to Stowe carry on about himself, he had reached the same conclusion. Her astuteness impressed him. "He enjoys the chase, the game. I made him every promise the East India Company expects me to make, and I had a sense I was wasting my breath."

Her eyes lifted to his. "I don't know if my father will see matters the way we do."

To the devil with Russell Tarleton. Fyclan had her to himself, and he didn't want to waste the time discussing old feuds or lost books.

And so he spoke of what he'd never shared with anyone before.

"My Gran was a gypsy. She married an Irish soldier and said she had no regrets although there were those who shunned her. She held no grudges. She said there was not enough time in life to waste on little minds."

"She is right," Miss Tarleton murmured.

"When I asked her why she had been willing to leave her people for my grandfather, even understanding how she would be treated in his world, she said it was because he had been her destiny."

Miss Tarleton's head tilted as if she was listening but held reservations.

"Gran told me that someday I, too, would meet my destiny. She said when I saw her, I would know—immediately." He let his words sink before saying, "Today, you walked past me on the street, and I knew."

Her chin lifted in doubt.

"I know you've heard pretty words like this before," he

said. "You've been flattered and feted and given every accolade a man can offer to earn your attention, but I want you to understand, that even as lovely as you are—and you are beautiful, Jennifer—" He used her given name. It sounded right. It *was* right. "—What I noticed was the determination in your step. And then to discover your intelligence, your sense of independence . . . you are the one."

She shifted her weight away from him. "You flatter me with your attention, sir—"

With an angry swipe of his hand through the air, Fyclan cut her off. "I'm *not* speaking platitudes.

"You would be beautiful to me even if you were as ugly as a crone and wobbled like a duck."

He had to make her understand. He might not have another opportunity.

"My Gran had the gift of sight. She told me that I would be an important man. She had seen my fate in her dreams. She said that when I found 'the one,' I would love her for life, the same way she had loved my grandfather. She said I would willingly give up everything I own for her, that I would surrender my soul to her because we were meant to be together."

He took a step toward. "She also said I should not be afraid. All would be good for us. Our children's children would be dukes. They would create a new world, one that reflected the love we had for each other. She said I must trust this woman to take me into a new life."

Was she listening? Did he sound mad? He couldn't tell. He felt mad, crazed even. If she didn't understand, if she thought he was spouting foolishness, he didn't know what he would do.

She had gone still, her face pale in the moon's silvery light.

"When I saw you today, I believed. I followed you to Sir David's, and within moments of talking to you, I *knew* I'd found you."

The world beyond the two of them had receded. He heard no sound of German singing or the presence of others. There was only the night air and the beating of their hearts.

And then a tear rolled her cheek.

One tear, and Fyclan felt gutted. He did not know what it meant. He feared her answer.

She raised a hand, placing her fingers to her lips as if needing to steady herself before saying, "I am not the one."

Before he could deny her claim, she said, "I will not have children, Mr. Fyclan Morris. With me, you would have no descendants, let alone ducal ones. The truth is, I was never meant to live long. My heart is not strong. Mr. Higley, my family's physic, has warned I might not survive childbirth." The tears were falling freely now. "That is one of the reasons I feel I'm an imposter. My family expects me to marry to rescue them from the debts Father has run up with his gaming. We are completely desperate. I play a charade of being an eligible wife for these titled men, but I'm not, except for perhaps someone like Stowe who already has his heirs and is now looking for a beautiful second wife, an ornament to show off at balls. I'm a fraud."

Her torrent of words caught him off guard. Her confession scrambled everything he had believed, and yet, he knew *he wasn't wrong in what he felt for her.*

But before he could form the words to calm both their fears, she took his silence for rejection. Lowering her head in shame, she ran for the door.

Her hand was on the door handle when he hooked his hand around her arm and swung her to him. He grabbed her arms, holding her so that he could look into her eyes. "*Believe*," he said. One word. One important word. "You must believe."

"In what?" The words came out in tears. She was breaking into pieces, and he was in danger of losing her.

"In *me. In us.* In love. "

Her lips parted. She appeared ready to throw his plea back in his face. Her eyes, full of hurt, searched his, then whispered. "Can it be that simple?"

"Yes," Fyclan said, relief flooding him. "*Yes.*"

And then, because it was right, because it was the most honest action he'd ever taken, he kissed her.

Her lips tasted of salt. They were wet and still trembled, but she did not pull away.

He breathed into her all his strength, all of his certainty. His arms threaded through hers. Her shaking stopped. Her lips softened, and the kiss deepened.

Had he ever kissed before? He thought not. She was the moonlight and the blood thundering through his veins. She filled his arms and his heart, and he knew it would take a lifetime to understand her, a lifetime well spent.

She was *the one.*

A sound behind him was the only warning before the door was thrown open, and Colonel Tarleton said, "*What the devil?*"

"Colonel, please, don't make a scene," an anxious woman's voice said.

The kiss broke. Fyclan swiftly faced Tarleton, protecting Jennifer with his body.

Her mother hovered in the doorway behind her angry husband. There were two young women there as well. They must be her sisters.

This was not the way Fyclan had planned on presenting himself to her family. He'd known that Tarleton would never approve a match between him and his daughter unless there was a great deal of money involved—and he was ready to pay. After all, Tarleton was an opportunist. Fyclan dealt with such men every day.

However, Fate had dealt a different hand.

"Jenny, go to your mother," the colonel ordered. She held back, almost as if frightened.

"We need to speak," Fyclan said. "My intentions are honorable."

"Your intentions?" Tarleton laughed at the words. "You touch her again, and I will call you out."

For a second, Fyclan was tempted. He wasn't afraid of Tarleton or dueling. He knew he would win because Jennifer was his although there had been a time he wouldn't have minded putting a hole in Colonel Tarleton just for the sake of the action.

Except, now, his only concern was for Jennifer. No good would come of his shooting her father.

And so he let her go. She moved past him, her head down. She slipped around the door, and he watched as her mother and sisters enveloped her. Her mother glanced up and down the hall as if worried someone would notice what was happening. The German was still singing.

"You will never touch my daughter again," Tarleton said.

"How much?" Fyclan answered. "You are trying to marry her off for money. How much do you want? Name your price."

Greed lit the colonel's face, and then he shook his head. "You are a nobody. One word in the right ear, such as Lord Stowe's, and the directors of the East India Company would give you the booting you so richly deserve."

"As they did you?" Fyclan couldn't stop himself. After all, he was Irish. He didn't back away from a fight.

"You wanted that command for yourself," Tarleton answered.

"I believed the men deserved leadership that would win without needlessly costing lives."

"That is what a *military* man is for."

"Interesting," Fyclan said, measuring his voice. "I remember you stayed well behind the 'battle' lines."

"I was in command."

"I said *well* behind the battle lines, and a number of knowledgeable, high-placed men, including officers, agreed with me."

Tarleton's hand went to his hip as if to pull a sword that was not there. Fyclan waited to be called out. Yes, he wanted Jennifer, but he was not one to deny the decisions he made in Calcutta to win her. Good men had died under Tarleton for the wrong reasons.

Abruptly, the colonel turned to the door. He paused. "Never," he promised. "You will *never* have her." He left.

Fyclan stayed a long time in the night's darkness, deciding his next move.

Tarleton was wrong. Fate had been set in motion. Fyclan would not lose his Jenny.

Chapter Seven

THE RIDE HOME in the hired conveyance was tense.

Jenny's sisters were not certain what was wrong, but they sat cowed, as did their mother, who had a worried air.

The colonel's back was straight. A clenched fist rested on his knee.

There would be a reckoning . . . however, Jenny was not afraid. She had done nothing of which to be ashamed. She also wondered about what would have set her father so completely against Fyclan Morris.

When they arrived home, Jenny started up the stairs with her mother and sisters, but her father stopped her. "Let us speak in the sitting room. Join us, Isabel," he said to her mother.

He shut the door behind the women after they entered the room. Her mother chose to sit in a side chair, but Jenny stood in the middle of the room, braced for whatever her father had for her.

The set of his mouth grim, her father said, "Fyclan Morris is a scoundrel. He has tried to ruin me with lies and innuendo. I would not have you give countenance to anything the man says."

"What is the bad blood between you, Father?"

"Jealousy. Morris is not a military man. He doesn't understand the workings of the military mind. Because he wanted to impress his superiors in the East India Company, he did all he could to undercut me. I will not have him use my daughter against me."

"I would not allow him to do so, Father."

He nodded his satisfaction. He seemed pleased, so she dared to ask questions.

"Will you not tell me, sir, exactly his offenses against you?"

Her father reared back as if she had slapped him. "This is not a matter for discussion. You have a role in this family, missy, and that is to do what your mother and I wish of you. We have all made considerable sacrifices for your benefit."

"And I appreciate them," Jenny answered. "Although I understand you expect something in return."

"Expect something?" A dangerous note crept into his tone, but Jenny wasn't afraid. Resentment was brewing a hot bile inside her.

"You expect me to marry for a title and money," she pointed out.

"As does every other parent presenting a daughter for marriage," the colonel answered.

"I think not. Their families have resources. We are

done up, and if I don't marry for money, you'll be in prison and mother and my sisters shamed."

The words had poured out of her. Unwise words. But she could not stop herself. "Mr. Morris won't ruin you, Father. You are doing a fine job yourself—"

The slap of his hand stopped her.

For a long moment, the ugly sound lingered in the air. Her skin stung where he had hit her. Hot tears came to her eyes but not out of fear or pain, but anger.

Jenny knew he was within his rights. He was male. He had all the power. He could beat her if he so desired.

What did surprise her was how the core of resentment inside her held firm. She clenched her hands at her side.

Her mother had jumped to her feet in alarm but made no move to come to Jenny's aid.

"You will have nothing to do with Morris," her father ordered in the silence. "If he comes sniffing around, you will tell me."

She gripped her fists tighter, her nails digging into her palms. "Yes . . . Father," she said, adding the last because she'd learned he expected it. He had returned from India after years of not even writing and commanded immediate obedience. He'd ruined her family, she realized. Before, when they'd lived in their modest home in Lansdown, they'd had no expectations and had been content. Then he had taken over their lives with his plan to sell Jenny off into marriage. She was nothing to him. None of them meant anything to him.

If she'd had doubts about Fyclan Morris before, they evaporated.

"Your mother said you believe Stowe won't come up to scratch. You are wrong. You women think we men have nothing to do with our time except moon over you. Someone writes a few poems to the lobe of your ear, and you imagine you have power. Well, you don't, daughter. You do what *I* say. Stowe is going to make an offer. The Duke of Gillingham is as well. Ha! See, you didn't know that."

He pointed his long finger at her nose in triumph. "You claim all I do is gamble. You are wrong. I was in the gaming room working for you. Gillingham expressed interest in you to me tonight. You see, I know men. There is a competition going on among them for you, and I am playing it." He tapped the side of her head with two fingers. "Don't think, Jenny. It doesn't suit you. Smile, dance, and say what I want you to say."

And if I don't?

She didn't utter the words. They would provoke him further.

He glared as if pretending to read her mind, but he couldn't. Her face was a mask.

"Very well," he said, taking her quietness for obedience. "Go to your room. Tomorrow, you will have callers. I know this. Be prepared to charm them."

Jenny went to her room, wanting to grind her teeth over the injustice of her life. She had once been close to her sisters. However, their father's ambitions had altered them. They reacted as if everything of value to them would be taken, and for Serena especially, that was correct. She blamed Jenny that Squire Paulson had become set against her.

However, Jenny wondered if the good and sensible squire wasn't more concerned over his son's marrying into the family of a notable gambler than his claims of needing a dowry. The squire had held no doubts about a match between Serena and Evan in the months of their courtship before the colonel had returned.

Their mother, too, had changed. There had been a time when she'd made the decisions. Now, she behaved as a mouse, nodding as the colonel issued dictates.

He would marry Jenny off as quickly as he could . . . to anyone but Fyclan Morris.

Mandy was waiting to help Jenny undress. The maid had picked up the mood in the house. She was not her usual talkative self, and that was fine with Jenny. She climbed into bed, but she lay awake for a long time, reliving those precious moments of conversation with Mr. Morris.

And that kiss—

What a perfect kiss. She had told him the truth about herself, and he hadn't backed away. Instead, he had wrapped her in his arms and for the space of a few moments, she had felt precious and protected. They hadn't shared just any kiss. Fyclan's kiss had been a pledge, a promise.

It would also be the last kiss she'd ever have from him. Her father was not a man to cross. He meant what he'd said. He would see her a spinster before letting her be with Fyclan.

As for Sir David's journal, she would have to see how she could maneuver her father into letting her return it.

Perhaps her mother would help. At the same time, Jenny never wanted to let go of the book. It would be her one, and probably last, connection to the first man she'd met whom she could love.

Had she thought her heart weak before?

Nothing in her life compared to the feeling of loss she suffered now.

When she finally fell asleep, she dreamed, something she rarely did. She found herself walking through an important house. She could tell by its size and the furnishings. They were rich and stately. There was an inviting fire in the hearth of the sitting room.

Entering the room, Jenny noticed the portrait over the mantel. It was she—no, the picture *wasn't* of her. The woman had black hair, yet her features were reminiscent of Jenny's.

In the dream, Jenny stepped back and the thought went through her that this was her daughter. Her lovely daughter dressed as if she was a duchess. *A child of her own—*

The realization startled her awake.

Jenny sat up. She was in her room. She looked around in the darkness and let the tears fall, tears for a daughter she would never have.

THE NEXT AFTERNOON, Alice opened Jenny's door without knocking. "A messenger is here with a package for you."

Jenny and Mandy had been strategizing over how to refashion the cream dress for a ball that night. "Is it flowers?" If so, Lorry could just put them in the sitting room so that whoever sent them could see that his gift was appreciated when he called.

"If you wish to know, find out for yourself," her sister said crossly. "The messenger is still cooling his heels downstairs. Won't leave until he gives you his package." She left.

Curious, Jenny went downstairs. The colonel was still at home. He had just been finishing his breakfast. He was wigless but dressed for the day. He stood in the hallway, suspiciously frowning at the tall man by the door, whom Jenny recognized immediately. *Childs.*

The manservant held a package. Upon seeing her, he bowed. "Miss Tarleton, your neighbor, my mistress, sent these for your enjoyment."

But as Jenny knew, there was no neighbor lady. These books had to be from Mr. Morris.

She broke open the string and unwrapped the paper. There were three books. One fiction, one a study of flora in Wales, and another was the account of Sir David's first trip to India.

The colonel snorted his opinion. "Books." But he didn't take them away from her. She had no doubt he could, but for whatever blessing, he hadn't.

"I'm to come here and pick up what you've read every day, Miss," Childs said as if quoting a script. "My mistress appreciates that you admire her library."

Jenny was tempted to cry "Hosanna" at such a generous offer. How clever of Mr. Morris to choose this way to retrieve the book she'd borrowed yesterday. Keeping her features carefully schooled, she turned to the colonel. "Father, may I give Mrs. Rockwell's book to her servant?"

"The one I took yesterday?"

"Yes, sir."

He debated for a moment, then, with a world-weary sigh, went upstairs. A few minutes later, Lorry, who also acted as his valet, came down with the book.

Jenny was thankful her father was in his room. She handed the journal to Childs. "Tell Mrs. Rockwell that I deeply appreciate her sending me these books."

"I shall return on the morrow for any you don't wish to read or have finished," Childs answered, his face impassive.

"Thank you," she said, and he took his leave.

She carried her precious books up the stairs. The colonel was in the hallway, both wig and jacket on. Her mother was there as well.

Seeing Jenny's hand stroke the cover of one of the books as she came up the stairs, he turned disgruntled. "I don't know if your schedule will give you time to read."

For once, her mother spoke up. "If our daughter finds pleasure in reading, then it is good."

He muttered something and went on his way.

Jenny hurried to the privacy of her room because she had noticed something inside one of the books, something she'd hoped no one else in the hallway had caught a glimpse of—a letter.

She now slipped it from the pages. The envelope was heavy. There was no name on the outside, but the wax seal was fresh. She broke it, knowing before she saw his name penned at the end of the letter that it was from Fyclan . . .

Chapter Eight

Dear Miss Tarleton,

Please pardon this unusual method of calling upon you. Obviously, my suit for your hand is not acceptable to your father. Furthermore, you have a number of eligible, wealthy, titled gentlemen vying for your hand.

The word "vying" made Jenny smile.

I understand your father's concerns. If my daughter had gained the interest of some of the most important men in London, I, too, would frown upon an Irishman like myself. However, I want to assure you that my intentions are true. Our paths were meant to cross. I wish to marry you, to cherish you, and to build a life with you.

Before you accuse me of making such a claim

*without knowing you, understand that is the purpose
of this letter. I fear that an officer of the East India
Company, a relative nobody until he is fortunate or
canny enough to receive a directorship, would make a
poor showing among your suitors.*

*But here, in the privacy of the written word,
sharing a passion we both share, namely books,
perhaps you will allow me to know you better. Perhaps
you will even come to know me.*

*You are more than just a lovely woman, Miss
Tarleton. You have imagination, a quality I value.*

I hope in time, you will see in me value as well.

*If it is your wish to continue correspondence, place
your letter in one of the books. Childs will come daily
with packages from Sir David's library for you. Place
your letter in one of them, and he will return it to me.*

I have one more request. Please, <u>believe</u>.

*I've spent the night thinking about your doctor and
his verdict on your heart. I don't disagree with what
he says. He should know better than I. However, my
experiences in life have taught me that there is very
little we truly know about the workings of mind and
body. I know you are destined for a wonderful life. I
believe you have a great heart. Our children will be
beautiful.*

He then wrote about a funny scene he'd witnessed that
morning as he'd walked to work. A cart overloaded with
chickens headed for market or as he'd written, "headed
for their beheadings," had lost a wheel and fallen over

on its side right in front of Westminster Hall. Several of the cages holding the chickens had broken, and the birds had raced madly for freedom until they caught sight of an orange girl selling her fruit on the corner and decided they wished to break their fasts and had attacked. *Ferocious chickens,* he declared.

Jenny couldn't help but smile at the word pictures he created out of the chaos. She could imagine how those hurrying importantly around Westminster would appreciate chickens on the loose.

She smoothed the foolscap around his bold signature, "Fyclan," imagining him dipping his nib in ink and penning this story for her. A silly story. Not one of importance . . . but she was charmed.

His sense that she would prefer books to a hundred dozen roses was correct.

She reread the letter, four or five times. She tucked it back into the book, walked around the room, then backed away.

A knock on the door interrupted her. Mandy's awed voice said, "Miss Jenny, Lord Stowe and His Grace, the Duke of Gillingham have come calling. They appeared at the same time. The duke has flowers."

Good. Their appearance saved her from making a rash decision. Her father would be furious if he found the letter, and who knew what he would do if he discovered she'd replied?

But when she joined her mother and her noble suitors, she couldn't take her mind off the scene with chickens racing through the streets. Lord Stowe thought her amusement was in response to some witticism of his, something she hadn't even heard.

That night, she attended the ball with her family. Another suitor threw his hand in the fray. The Earl of Dumberton was even older than the duke or Stowe and from one of the oldest families in England. He pronounced himself smitten by her beauty, and she could almost see the gentlemen present in the room planning the wagers they would place in Brooks's betting book. The stakes were now higher than ever. Three noble, wealthy gentleman were paying her court . . . what more could any woman ask?

And she knew the answer.

When Jenny returned home, she did write a letter to Mr. Morris. She could not stop herself.

She even dared to sign herself *Jenny*.

Her letter was not particularly interesting. She thanked him for the books and wrote about the ball . . . but it was a start.

Childs arrived the next day as promised with another package for her. The colonel was not at home this time. Jenny had a book with her letter in it ready to be returned. She was very pleased to see that Fyclan had kindly written to her again.

In the sanctuary of her bedroom, she pored over every word. He wrote in this letter about his adventures in India and how he hoped soon to be named a director with the Company. He was presenting his prospects to her. The thought gladdened her soul.

She had not imagined him an adventurer, yet he had

fought the Marathas. He didn't speak of war. Instead, he talked of the animals he'd seen with such vivid descriptions she could almost feel the hot breath of the tiger he'd once confronted or smell the monkeys. They had stolen his shaving kit: *They wanted the glass in it and spent hours in the trees not far from my window gazing at their perfect reflections.*

Jenny had to write him back. She had no choice. She was full of questions.

And thus it began and grew.

Meanwhile, the very public race for her hand was on. She no longer cared. She didn't even worry about gambling debts or her sisters' prospects. She smiled and nodded at the appropriate time for suitors or when she went out into society—but *herself* she saved for her letters.

Of course, all was not perfect. Her father's creditors were starting to come around. His questions about marriage offers became strained. He took to staying at home in the afternoons so that he could be present for her callers.

In turn, the gentlemen, even the duke, were not pleased with his presence and the amount of her father's gambling debts. Jenny had overheard a reference to them more than once.

Serena had taken to acting as if she were in mourning. She was certain Evan had forgotten her. She worried that he was in Lansdown, planning to wed his cousin.

And Alice was surly. She rambled incessantly about her husband's need to purchase a promotion so that his brilliance would be recognized.

Their mother spent most of her day in her room.

Jenny became three people. For her family, she tried to appear smiling and flirtatious with her suitors. However, with the gentlemen, she was distant and a bit solemn. She discovered that men did not appreciate cold aloofness—any more than they did her father's blustery confidence.

Only with Fyclan was she true to herself.

Her letters moved beyond social niceties. She found herself writing about her family's disappointments and the changes in them since her father had returned home. All were secrets she should not share with an outsider. However, she had come to trust Fyclan.

He answered with sensitivity and wisdom. He assured her everything would be all right. She hoarded his letters, hid them carefully in a ripped seam in her mattress, re-reading them whenever she felt low.

I don't care what other people believe, she wrote. *It is your goodwill I consider. You have become the sun to the shadows in my day.*

He wrote back. *Then know that my admiration and respect for you have only grown stronger with each passing moment. If I am the sun, then you are the moon. I am not good at flowery language. Let me state my case clearly—I cannot imagine my life without you.*

Jenny stared at his last sentence. She felt the same. Others wooed her with flowers and wealth. Fyclan courted her with words and honest emotion.

She dreamed of the portrait room almost every night. Each time, the dream was more vivid, more real. She began wondering if Mr. Higley might have been wrong. After all, her skin was smooth and cream-colored, not the blue of her birth or early childhood. Perhaps she had outgrown any malady. She even felt strong. Was the dream not a sign that she might have children?

Hope is a fragile thing, but she discovered it can quickly grow into conviction. And she found she wanted to believe, desperately so. Her arms ached to hold a child of her own making. Her soul yearned to trust that she could have a full and complete life.

Nor did she wish to marry an old man, not when another held her heart.

Soon, she lulled herself into trusting that all would work in her favor. It must. She was in love with Fyclan Morris, and didn't people belong with those they loved? Isn't that what the poets lauded? Didn't their letters to each other prove love in its highest form?

She prayed it was true.

However, in spite her hopes for a miracle, she found herself completely unprepared when there was a knock on the front door moments after her family finished an early supper. They would be going out for another rout, another opportunity to lure in Stowe or the others. Jenny was heartily tired of the game.

She was on the stairs, ready to go to her room before leaving, when Lorry opened the door. She glanced back in curiosity and was startled to see Fyclan standing there.

For a second, she feared she would collapse. He appeared extraordinarily handsome in a jacket of deepest blue velvet and white evening breeches. His black hair was pulled back and tied at the nape of his neck. He held his hat under his arm.

She took a step down the stairs toward him while her father charged forth.

"How dare you place yourself on my doorstep, Morris." He would have slammed the door in Fyclan's face except the Irishman raised a rock-hard arm to stop him.

"You need to hear me out."

"I need nothing from you."

"Tarleton, I'm not here to fight." He offered a leather packet that he had been carrying. "These are your gambling vowels." He referred to the slips of paper her father had signed acknowledging his debts.

"What are you doing with them?" The colonel's knuckles tuned white as his hand tightened its grip on the door.

"Giving them to you."

"*Why?*"

"May I come in to discuss this?"

"*No.* State your purpose and begone.

Fyclan's gaze slid to meet Jenny's. "I am here to ask for your daughter's hand in marriage."

Before her father could speak, Jenny said, "*Yes.* Yes, yes, and yes."

Chapter Nine

_____

W HEN F YCLAN STATED his purpose, he'd watched Jenny because she was the only one who mattered.

Her eyes had widened at his proposal, then the words had poured out of her.

She would have launched herself from the step toward him, and he was ready for her. He'd waited eagerly for her letters but he wanted, no, needed her presence, in his arms, in his bed, and in his life.

For two weeks he'd been pacing the floor of his room wondering what she was doing, how she was being treated, whether she was happy. He hated that other men could call on her, and, finally, he'd realized that if he wanted Tarleton to take him seriously, then he must step forward.

It had been no trick at all to collect the colonel's gaming debts. His debtors were happy to release them. They had doubted if Tarleton would ever pay. Some believed that, even if he did find a wealthy lord for his daughter, those gentlemen wouldn't be as generous as Tarleton expected them to be. After all, Stowe and the others were not fools. Why should they pay another man's debts?

Hearing this made Fyclan all the more determined to claim her. He would not allow a star as bright and sparkling as Jenny to be gossip fodder.

Now, she reached for him, her happy "yes" ringing in his ears, her eyes full of joy—but her father blocked her path.

"*No.* I forbid it. No daughter of mine will accept the likes of you, Morris."

"Are you going to give him back your gambling debts, Father?" Jenny challenged.

Tarleton held up the packet. "They've been handed to me. They are mine. Morris knows he should never have given them over."

"They are a gift," Fyclan answered. "You wish to barter your daughter's hand for money. I have money. What is the cost?"

Before Tarleton could open his mouth, one of Jenny's sisters came forward. "I want advancement for my husband," she said anxiously.

"I want everything that Jenny has received," the other said. "I want to be presented for a Season and wear the finest clothes and I want my own bedroom. And a dowry. I want a good dowry."

It was clear that marrying Jenny wasn't going to be an inexpensive proposition.

Fyclan could see that same thought in her worried

eyes, and he wanted to laugh out loud. She had nothing to worry over. His fortune rivaled Stowe's and was of his own making.

Well, he *had* a fortune. The Tarletons seemed bent on taking a huge amount of it, but he didn't care. He'd been waiting for Jenny all of his life—

"You'll not be receiving anything from him," Tarleton told his daughters, "because I would never let an Irish scoundrel touch any of you." He scowled at Fyclan. "I prayed to someday put you in your place, Morris, and the time has come. You aren't fit to polish my boots, and I'll not have you in my family no matter how much money you wish to wave in front of me."

"Don't you believe your daughter has something to say in the matter?"

Tarleton snorted his opinion. "My daughters do what I tell them. My Jenny is going to be a fine lady. A marchioness or a duchess. That is one thing your money can't buy. Now be gone." He slammed the door in Fyclan's face.

And, of course, the bastard had kept the gaming vowels.

But Fyclan wasn't discouraged yet. He had done what was honorable. Regardless of what Tarleton believed, Jenny was going to be his wife. His Gran had seen it. Her gift never lied.

He walked down the steps.

The hour was the soft light just before the sun set. He knew Tarleton watched him from a window in the house. He walked to the corner and turned down the side street. He followed his instinct and took an alleyway behind the row of houses.

Jenny's voice rang in his ear, *Yes. Yes, yes, and yes.* She knew her own mind. She was fire and lightning. No man could cow her, not even her own father.

And then there she was.

Jenny stepped through a gate behind one of the houses and into the alley. She was hatless and didn't wear gloves.

For a second, he feared his eyes deceived him, and then she came *running* to him.

She threw her arms around him. She smelled of the spring air and her own delicate, wonderful scent, and he wasn't about to ever let her go.

He kissed her, right there for all to see if they'd had a mind to, but she ended it quickly.

"We must hurry," she warned. "Father will soon know I've left—that is, if you will have me after all his angry words?"

He started to declare his love but she placed her fingers on his lips. "I warn you, Fyclan, I am coming to you with nothing but the clothes I'm wearing. I told him I needed to return to my room for something, then I went down the servants' stairway."

"You are all I want," he said. "All I've ever wanted. And, of course, you are right—your father will want my head, but it doesn't matter. Nothing matters except that you have chosen me. Come then." He took her hand. He led her in a direction that he didn't believe Tarleton would think to search first. After all, he'd learned in India that Colonel Tarleton was not the most resourceful of men. However, his daughter was his prized possession.

Or so he'd claimed.

"Where are we going?" Jenny asked.

"Scotland."

She came to a halt. "We are eloping?"

Fyclan recognized his mistake. If he was going to take on a wife as quick as Jenny, he needed to start talking to her instead of keeping his plans in his head. "I meant what I said. I want you for my wife."

She wavered a moment.

"You can return," he said, even though the words felt as if he was ripping his heart from his chest.

"No, I can't. The moment I walked out of the house, I threw my lot in with you. It is just that it give me a moment's pause to think of leaving my mother, my sisters. Father won't take this well."

"He will not."

"They might not as well."

"If it is the eloping, we can try and think of another way."

In day's fading light, she gave him a smile, a brave one that said she was uncertain of the future, yet chose to go forward. "There is no other way. You are right. There will be anger, but I believe I'm in love with you, Fyclan Morris."

"I *know* I'm in love with you, Jennifer Tarleton."

"Love is enough, isn't it?"

"It will be for us." He held out his hand. "And we will stare them all down."

She placed her palm in his. They laced their fingers together. "When you came to the door, I realized I didn't want to live if living meant not being with you. And that isn't a prophecy, Fyclan, it is the yearnings of my own heart."

"You will never regret your choice, Jenny."

She laughed. "I'm not worried about that, Fyclan. I fear you may be the one with regrets."

"Never."

"I shall hold you to that, sir."

And he was fine with the challenge.

He found a vehicle for hire and had them driven to the Lion's Head, a coaching inn. There he made arrangements for a post chaise, a fast team, and postboys to drive them to Scotland.

She didn't waver in her decision again, and, within the hour, they found themselves traveling north.

THE TRIP TOOK almost three full days. Fyclan did not let them stop except for meals. He thought her father might follow, but Jenny suspected differently.

Her father wasn't one for defiance. His gaming debts were settled, so what more did he need? Fyclan had done what Tarleton would have asked her husband to do.

She was somewhat curious as to the amount of those debts but didn't ask. However, between the settlement and the expense of the horses for their trip to Scotland, she was gaining a healthy respect for Fyclan's financial standing.

She knew he worked. Then again, she'd heard that while many of the men in service with the East India Company were very wealthy, others not so much.

"Does your employer know you've left?" she asked Fyclan. They had just changed the horses and were on their way.

"I imagine your father has told them."

"Will they be upset?"

Fyclan sat back in the seat. The weather was good for travel. He'd taken off his coat, and he now put his arm around her.

The first time he'd done it, she'd been quite shy and very conscious of the postboy riding the team of horses. Still, it felt good to be this close to him. His shoulders were strong and muscular. She liked resting against his chest. He seemed completely at ease with her but respectful. She appreciated his patience because, even though she had been raised in the country, she was uncertain what was expected.

Human mating couldn't be like two sheep, could it? She hoped not.

However, in Fyclan's arms, she felt safe.

"I may be asked to leave," Fyclan said, "but if I am, I have no regrets. We'll be fine."

"I know we will. I'd live in a hut with you, Fyclan, and I'll have you understand, I know a bit about cooking. I won't kill you with it."

He laughed, pleased.

After their first stop, he had returned to the chaise with a deck of cards and had quickly learned her father wasn't the only gambler in the family, or so Fyclan claimed. They spent hours trying to best each other at piquet and vingt-et-un.

"I'm discovering you are *not* a gambler," she accused back.

"Quite true," he admitted.

"Then how do you make your money?"

He shuffled the cards a moment before saying, "With careful study. I don't hope, I *know* what the return will be before I use my money."

"And you have never lost money?"

"A time or two. I do not use money that I can't afford to lose. That is my first rule."

The rule made sense. Her father hadn't been able to afford any of the money he lost.

They didn't stop to rest. Fyclan opened his arm, an invitation for her to snuggle against him that she couldn't resist. Of course, the first night of their travel, she'd been tense. She'd sat away from him in the close confines in the chaise. However, now she was more comfortable. She was becoming familiar enough with him to snuggle up.

And he was pleased.

His lips brushed the top of her hair. "I may have more money than Stowe and many others," Fyclan admitted. "But it wasn't until I had you in my arms that my life became rich."

Chapter Ten

THEY REACHED THE Scottish border in late afternoon. Gretna Green was only another nine miles, and the horses were fresh. When they arrived, they had no difficulty finding the blacksmith's shop.

The blacksmith, Joseph Paisley, took one look at them and knew what they wanted. He told them there was plenty of time left in the day for marrying, so why delay?

Fyclan and Jenny agreed, and the blacksmith offered Jenny the use of a private room to freshen up a bit.

"You can cool your heels under that tree waiting for her," Paisley told Fyclan, "although you look happily ready to take on married life."

He was right. Fyclan had always thought that a man besotted by love was a weak one.

He now knew the opposite was true.

He loved Jenny. Yes, she was a pleasing to look at, but it was her spirit that captivated him.

He adored the way she rolled her eyes before playing a card and giving away her intent. Or brought her brows together as she tried to analyze why he always knew her purpose.

He admired her strength of character. It had not been easy for her to walk away from her family, and yet she had done so to thrive.

And now, she was going to give herself to him.

She hadn't even known how wealthy he was.

Now, as he waited under a spreading yew at the blacksmith's shop at the center of Gretna Green, the first place over the Scottish border where lovers could marry quickly, he understood why bridegrooms were nervous. It was a heady thing to take a wife, but to claim one who so completely placed her trust in him was a weighted responsibility.

For the first time in his memory, he found himself praying. He hoped he was worthy of her. He was also anxious that no harm come to her. In three very close days of travel, Jenny had become the most important person in his life. He could not imagine going on without her.

So, what if childbirth did take her from him?

Fear of the story she told him about her heart rested heavy on his mind. He would do anything to care for her.

"I'm ready."

At the sound her voice, he turned, and was immediately taken back to that first moment when he'd seen her on the street and she'd captured his attention. Her blond hair like strands of sunlight flowed loose around her shoulders. Her blue eyes shone with love for him.

She held out her hand. "Are you ready?"

"I am overwhelmed," he said truthfully. "I will never tire of looking at you, especially when you are smiling as you are now."

Her laughter was light. "Come, my love."

With joined hands, they entered the blacksmith's shop. Paisley waited for them by the door. He was a canny Scotsman, one who expected to be paid well for his services, and once that was done, he took charge.

"Stand here," he ordered, placing them in front of his anvil with their hands joined on the cold iron. When they were in position, he didn't waste time. He said to Fyclan, "Do you wed this woman?"

"I do."

Paisley turned his stern features on Jenny. "And what of you? Will you take this man?"

Jenny tilted her head to Fyclan. They stood so close he could lean forward and kiss her. Her lips curved into an inviting smile. "I do," she said in her calm, measured voice. "But I have something else to add"

"Carry on," Paisley said. "It is your wedding."

She smiled into Fyclan's eyes, and said, "I love you as I could never love another. You have given me more than just your name. You have given the freedom to be myself. There is no gift more valuable."

Had any man ever received a greater compliment? And here, only minutes ago, he'd been anxious about the fragile nature of her life. She'd reminded him that one must always live fully and completely.

He kissed her then. This was not the considered,

sometimes devouring, kisses of the past days in the post chaise. He'd had a hard time keeping himself at bay.

No, this kiss was his promise to cherish her as she deserved. To hold her close as helpmate. To honor her as she honored him.

"Hey now," Paisley said. "I've not named you husband and wife, yet."

Fyclan broke the kiss long enough to say, "Then you'd best move on with it."

"I name you husband and wife," Paisley said. He brought his hammer down on his anvil, and Fyclan swept Jenny up in his arms.

"You may kiss your bride," Paisley finished, but Fyclan was already too busy kissing Jenny to pay him much mind.

THEY TOOK A room in Gretna Hall. Fyclan had let her have some privacy before he joined her in the bed.

Jenny was nervous. She had bathed, using the washbowl, and had combed her hair with her fingers. The hour was still early, the sun had not yet set.

If this had been her wedding night in London, she would have been pampered by Mandy and had a nightdress to wear. She had nothing here, so she wore her chemise and petticoats. They were so sheer, she felt practically naked, yet she had a feeling Fyclan would not object.

She hoped he wasn't disappointed in her for many reasons. She'd overheard her sister Alice complaining with some women friends that fulfilling marital duties was a chore. Jenny hoped not.

Kissing Fyclan was better than breathing. She'd come to yearn for his touch and the scent of his skin. She believed there was nothing finer in the world than to have him by her side. She'd not even realized how lonely she'd been until the day she'd met him in the library and had recognized a kindred soul.

After their letters and traveling with him in the confines of the coach, she understood him very well, and she knew he had some grave concerns. He thought about her heart, about her expectations and fear of death, and she knew she was the only one who could set his worries to rest—or make them worse.

There was a knock on the door.

She'd been sitting on the bed with her legs tucked beneath her. The mattress was lumpy. After nights spent sleeping in Fyclan's arms, Jenny didn't know if she wanted wool-stuffed bedding. She unfolded her legs and stood.

"Yes?" she said.

"May I come in?" Fyclan asked. He sounded so formal.

Here was the moment.

She crossed to the door. She could feel his presence on the other side, and she thought of their letters. She placed her hand on the cool wood. They had said so much to each other without the danger of confrontation. She wished she could write him now and tell him not to worry.

The letters had taught her that some things were easier to say in writing . . . or when one didn't need pretense.

So, she did not open the door. Instead she leaned close

to it, and said, "Do you know how deeply I love you?"

He had not been expecting her words. He had been waiting for a door to open.

Another man on his wedding night might demand the door be opened and enough with talking, a man who didn't care for her or who considered that she had a thought or opinion of her own.

Fyclan was not that man.

She could feel him move closer to her. "If it is half of what I feel for you, then no ocean could hold it."

Jenny smiled, loving the melodic sound of his voice.

She spoke from her heart. "You have changed my life. I once feared everything, did you know that? I was always conscious of being different. I was more a doll than a woman. I believed them when they told me I was frail, that I had no right to want more.

"And then you came into my life. I'd yet to meet a man who spoke to me as an equal, who valued what I had to say. And we shared a dream together—"

"Jenny, I would die myself if anything happened to you."

There it was, his fear. "I'm not fragile. I will not break," she whispered, knowing for the first time in her heart it was true. She wanted to live, to enjoy life fully.

"But what if being with child was too much for you—"

Jenny threw open the door.

He stood there as if lost.

She reached out and placed her hand against his jaw. "So handsome and so sad. I could feel it coming to you. Don't be afraid, Fyclan. Love me."

Before he could speak, she wrapped her arms around his neck and kissed him with the fullness of her being.

He kissed back, moving her into the room and kicking the door closed. This was what she wanted. All, she realized, she'd ever wanted. A joining, a meshing of two souls.

He broke the kiss, his voice harsh. "If anything happens to you because of my lust."

She held his face so that he must meet her eye. "You gave me a dream of a child who would become a great woman. This afternoon, you made me a promise that we would be one. I'll not settle for anything less, Fyclan Morris, than what you pledged to this marriage. Whether I die tomorrow or next year or decades from now, I want to live knowing that I've tasted everything life has to offer—including loving my husband in a manner that will make the heavens sing. Have no fear," she urged him, running her palm along the breadth of his shoulder. "The love I feel for you will always be there, even after death. But for today, let us live as lovers."

She kissed him then, and he responded openly and generously. He lifted her up and carried her to the bed, his hands already untying her lacings. She pushed his jacket down his arms, hampering his efforts. He shook his coat off, anxious to return to her. She pulled his shirt out and slid her hands beneath it, feeling the contours of hard muscles. They were clumsy, they were silly, and yet they had the same goal.

"Jenny," he whispered, breathing her name as if it were a benediction. He began kissing her nose, her eyes, her hair, and, finally, her mouth.

Live. She wanted to live, and in this moment she was. They were two people hungry for each other. His touch was magic. He knew what pleased her. He kissed the sensitive skin beneath her jaw and tickled a line to her ear.

He had her undressed first. Her fine lawn of her undergarments fell around her on the bed. He kissed the curve of her breasts. His kisses lowered until he touched her nipples—and she caught fire.

Her blood pounded in her veins. She had never realized they were so sensitive. Her heart, that very heart that so concerned everyone in her life, felt ready to burst with joy. Her fingers buried themselves in his thick hair.

At her touch, he started to stir as if alarmed. "Jenny, is this all right—?"

"*Don't stop.*" Now it was her turn to sound harsh. What Fyclan was doing with his mouth was the most delicious experience. Had he learned this in some exotic port of India? Or was it what every sensible Irishman knew?

She hoped it was the latter because, because truth be told, she would not want to rob any woman in the world of this pleasure.

And what pleased her even more is when she copied what he was doing to her. He liked when she nibbled his ear or the line of his throat. Her hands smoothed over his chest. His nipples were as tight as hers. She let her hand wander lower.

When he brought his hand down to hers, she thought he was going to stop her. Instead, he began unbuttoning his breeches. She pushed him aside, eager to do it herself as his mouth found hers again. This time, she tasted his tongue. Here was Temptation, especially when the back of her fingers brushed against the hardened length of him.

His shoes dropped to the floor as he kicked them off. She traced the curve of his buttocks as she pushed his breeches down. His hand flowed down to her waist and pulled her intimately to him.

Jenny hadn't realized her eyes were closed. She'd been too busy enjoying herself, learning him with her other senses. Now she opened them, and the love in his eyes threatened to overwhelm her.

"You're beautiful," he whispered.

"*You're* beautiful," she countered. "*This* is beautiful."

He grinned as he leaned her back on the bed, the weight of his body upon her. He brushed her hair from her temples. Deep within, she felt a need beginning to build. A pull he'd stirred into wakefulness when he had been teasing her breasts.

His hardness brushed against her, and she knew she undone. She opened her legs to him. "Please," she whispered, not even certain what she asked.

His mouth covered hers, and she felt him press toward the very core of her being.

For a second, she was startled. His shape was alien, yet her body quickly adjusted. In fact, she was a bit frustrated there wasn't *more*.

"Fyclan, if you don't do this, I fear I'll ignite from wanting you. I will."

He rose, and, in one smooth thrust, entered her. There was pain, but the pain was nothing compared to the wonder of understanding. This is what it meant to be joined to a man, to be one with him.

"Are you all right?" he asked, his voice anxious.

She looked him, stunned by the question. "Fyclan, make love to me."

And he did. He opened a new world to her. She had never dreamed of the bliss that came from this act of joining. How could anyone complain about this? It was joyful, exhilarating. The things he did to her body made her toes curl and her senses sing.

She moved with him. She could not hold back. She loved him so much, and now, this was just the grandest reward, and it seemed as if it would go on forever. She *hoped* it would go on forever. Her heart pounded in her ears, her brave, loving heart. She'd never been so proud of it.

Suddenly, her desire, her need burst inside her. She was no longer herself. He was all around her, and she was all around him.

Deep inside, she felt his seed fill her.

It was a miracle, she marveled. Their souls had actually become one.

Fyclan fell on the bed beside her. She turned to him, immediately missing his heat and that wickedly hard shaft that knew how to give her so much pleasure.

They were naked in a tumble of clothing. Fyclan shoved it all to the floor and flipped the counterpane to cover them. He moved closer, and she curled up next to him.

He pressed his lips to her temple. "Are you all right?" His tone was anxious.

She took his hand and rested it against her racing heart, right over her breast, the nipple still hard and swollen. "I have never been better." She lightly touched his crisp, black hair and tested her new name. "Mrs. Fyclan Morris."

"Are you happy?"

She nodded. "And so very pleased I didn't marry Lord Stowe. I don't believe he could have done that."

He laughed, the sound masculine and full, and she was filled with love for him. "He could never please you the way I can," he assured her, and she had no doubt that he was right.

She brought hand down to rest on her belly. She didn't feel a child had been created. Not yet. She thought of the portrait in her dreams. "Someday, I shall be a mother," she murmured. "I shall not fear the future."

He took her hand and kissed the back of her fingers. "I shall always protect you. Jenny, we shall see London doctors. They will know more than some country doctor."

She smiled, content for right now. And then she wondered, "So, do you think we might do that again?"

"You liked it?" There was hope in her husband's voice.

"I don't know." She pretended to frown. "I might need to try another sample."

Fyclan's answer was to gladly pull her into his arms and show her that, yes, they could do it as often as they wished.

Happily Ever After

THE COLONEL DISOWNED Jenny.

He was vocal and bombastic about it. His actions did not bother her. What hurt is that her mother and her sisters supported him, even after, once they'd returned from Scotland, Fyclan financed Alice's husband's advancement and settled a considerable dowry on Serena. She did not marry the squire's son but met a respectable barrister in Lansdown who helped her forget Evan. There were no thank-yous.

"Blood money," Serena had said, and for that, Jenny had no answer.

As for her mother? Well, she had waited years for her colonel husband to return home and could not go against him, or so she told her youngest daughter. Yes, he continued his reckless gambling, but what could a mere wife do? Jenny understood although her family's greed and choices saddened her.

What she did know is that being Mrs. Fyclan Morris suited her. She now understood the admonishment that when a man and woman married, they left their parents and became one. She was proud to stand beside her husband.

The letters they had once exchanged now served as a good foundation for their marriage. Of course, she had much more she needed to learn about Fyclan, and she delighted in the endeavor. Soon, she could reference his likes and dislikes and found him to be a kind and considerate helpmate, one who also happened to be very rich.

Indeed, apparently few had known how wealthy. "I was a bachelor," he explained to Jenny. "My needs were few, and I didn't want to miss a good investment."

Of course, Lord Stowe took exception to Fyclan's eloping with Jenny. He complained bitterly to the directors of the East India Company. They, in turn, let Fyclan go and were surprised when he set up his own firm of offices directly across the street. His friend John Bishard joined him, and together, they became Morris and Bishard.

No one particularly took notice of the new firm, until Jenny and Fyclan began building their house in Mayfair with a library that could one day rival Sir David's. Astute investors quickly learned that when it came to making money, Fyclan Morris had a gift. Very soon, his clients came only from the elite because he could afford to be selective. Eventually, even the East India Company looked to him for advice.

Jenny was not surprised to discover that, although her elopement caused a bit of a scandal at the time, doors were not closed to them. After all, there were those who sought Fyclan's attention to their personal fortunes. They didn't care that Fyclan was Irish. They wanted a sound return on their coin, and he always delivered.

In time, Mr. and Mrs. Morris were added to every guest list, including events at Court. He was one of the few that the king's advisors called upon regularly for his opinion.

Did it bother Jenny that her family had spurned her? Rarely. She discovered she was more resilient than anyone could have imagined.

She also didn't think about her heart. Her life was so full of happiness and love, she had no room for fear. She was too busy living each day to its fullest.

Her husband thought differently. Fyclan insisted that she be seen by the best doctors. They examined her coloring, asked if she had trouble breathing, or was tired—and then told him there was no medical way of determining how strong her heart was or wasn't. She appeared and acted fine. Yes, she rested every afternoon, but that was a reasonable action for a woman as active and busy as Jenny. In time, Fyclan, too, relaxed.

The only disappointment Jenny had was that she'd yet to be with child. It wasn't for lack of trying. She and her husband enjoyed their marriage bed. She feared the reason they didn't have children was because of her. Something had to be wrong with her.

Fyclan, who knew her moods so well, reminded her of his Gran's prediction and the dream Jenny had of the portrait. "Our children are destined for great things.

Look at what has happened to us. Please have faith, my love. Believe."

Then again, Fyclan trusted the future more easily than she did. He always had.

"I haven't had the dream since we were married," she answered. "What if it was all a fantasy?"

"Would my love for you be enough?" he asked.

Ah, there was the question. "At one time, before you, I accepted I might be childless. But you introduced me to hope. I yearn for a baby, Fyclan. My arms feel empty."

Nor did it help when she heard by way of others that Alice and Serena were each now proud mothers.

And then, on the fifth anniversary of their wild elopement to Gretna Green, Jenny had the dream again. This time the dream let her stand for what seemed to be as long as she wished in front of the portrait—her daughter, living evidence of the love Jenny and her husband shared.

Jenny woke with a start. She stared at the bedroom's darkness, needing a moment to understand her surroundings.

Attuned to his wife, Fyclan woke. "Is everything all right?" he murmured sleepily, drawing her close in his arms.

In answer, Jenny kissed him and, as things always went between them, they were soon making love. When they finished, Fyclan cradled her in his arms and fell back to sleep, but Jenny lay awake, a certain knowledge growing in her heart.

Three months later, she was not surprised to realize she was finally with child.

Jenny took to her bed. The doctors insisted. No one wanted to run the risk of losing Jenny's child. Fyclan told her that was because all of her doctors were half in love with her and didn't want to see her disappointed.

She doubted his words, but she would do anything for her baby.

Elin Grace Morris was born with curling black hair and eyes that the midwife assured Jenny would someday be as dark as her father's. She had ten fingers and ten toes and a bow-shaped mouth. She was the most beautiful baby Jenny had ever seen. Her name was chosen after Fyclan's Gran.

At last, Jenny had everything that gave her life purpose. She had a husband she adored and the child she had so desperately desired.

BUYING A COUNTRY estate had been Fyclan's idea. He chose a charming house located on the River Trent in Leicestershire. He called it Elin's christening present and Jenny thought it the perfect place for a girl to be happy. They named the estate Heartwood.

Their lives in London were busy, but here, even Fyclan could relax and enjoy the family. The estate was also adjacent to the seat of the Duke and Duchess of Baynton. The couples were fast friends in London. Her Grace was the mother of three sons, and Jenny had found her advice on motherhood invaluable.

Of course, when Fyclan and Jenny first arrived at Heartwood, the duke and duchess invited them almost immediately to Trenton, the name of the Baynton seat, for dinner.

Baynton and his wife greeted them enthusiastically when they arrived.

"Where are the boys?" Jenny asked.

"The twins are at school," Her Grace said. "Of course, and Ben will come down and join us for a bit. Are you happy with the house?"

"I adore it," Jenny said.

"Come in, come in," the duke invited.

Trenton was far grander than Heartwood. The noble family of Baynton had been in the service of the Crown for hundreds of years, and this estate was a testimony to their power.

It was also the manor in Jenny's dream.

She stood still in the hall, taking it all in. Elin wiggled in her arms, wishing to be let down. Jenny moved forward, walking past the receiving room, every detail like her dream. She stopped in the doorway of the sitting room.

There was a fire in the hearth, and over the mantel was the portrait of Marcella, the current duchess.

Did Fyclan understand? He was by her side. He took the baby from her and was watching Jenny closely.

Jenny turned to her husband. She could see that, yes, he understood. "Is this portrait like the one in your dreams?

She nodded. *The one.* "Except Elin is the duchess standing there." She knew it with certainty.

The duke and his wife had not noticed the exchange.

They were busy directing servants to set out refreshments for their guests. His Grace poured two healthy measures of amber whisky. He carried one over to Fyclan.

Her Grace offered Jenny a glass of Madeira. Jenny placed Elin on the thick India carpet and took a seat beside her friend. For a moment, the adults watched Elin look around the room with her bright intelligence, then try to stand.

Fyclan offered his hand to help her with her balance. She rewarded him with one of her sunny smiles.

The duke spoke. "Before we do anything else, Marcella and I have a matter we wish to discuss with you."

Jenny and Fyclan looked up with interest.

"You see," the duke continued, "I've been thinking about the conversation I had with you the last time we met, Fyclan. You are right, the world is changing. People with responsibilities such as mine should not leave important concerns to chance."

"That makes good sense," Fyclan said, helping Elin take a step, then another. She was going to run before she could walk.

"The old ways will not last," the duke said. "To survive, my title will need to think in modern terms. Too many of my noble friends are struggling with their finances."

Jenny knew that was true. Almost weekly, the gossip was about this young lord or that one wasting his fortune at gaming tables and on horses. Even if they were not foolish and gambled, those fortunes were becoming difficult to maintain, according to Fyclan, if all a family relied on was income from land to fill their coffers.

"I discussed this with Marcella, and we wish to propose to you a merger of sorts. We would like a marriage agreement between your daughter and my heir."

For a second, Jenny didn't believe she'd heard correctly. Fyclan also appeared stunned.

"I need you, Morris," the duke said, "to help steer my son Gavin in the right direction. But, please, this isn't just about the legacy of my title. Marcella and I value your friendship. I pray you say yes to our offer . . . which you should—that is, if you wish your grandsons to be dukes."

Jenny's gaze met Fyclan's. They both knew what the answer would be. Gavin Whitridge, a marquess in his own right although he was only eight, would make the perfect husband for Elin.

"Yes, of course," Fyclan said. "We are honored."

"Good," His Grace answered with a clap of hands. "That's settled."

Elin heard the sound and let go of her father's fingers to teeter on two sturdy legs and clap as well, a sign that she, too, was happy with her future. The adults laughed.

"Champagne," Her Grace announced. "I've had it waiting."

And so, as glasses were poured, Jenny found herself standing beside the mantel. Someday, Elin's picture would hang above it, and she knew the future was nothing to fear.

Not when it was filled with love.

Don't miss

THE MATCH OF THE CENTURY

the first full-length novel in Cathy's brand-new
Marrying the Duke **series!**

Coming November 24, 2015!

Read on for a sneak peek . . .

*In honor of Miss Elin Morris and her
parents Mr. and Mrs. Fyclan Morris
Gavin Whitridge, the Duke of Baynton and
Marcella, The Dowager Duchess of Baynton
request your presence at a ball
Tuesday, 11 April, 1809.
Dances begin at 10 p.m.
An Announcement of Great Importance
will be made before midnight.
A cold supper will be provided.
R.S.V.P. Menheim House*

Chapter One

ALL OF LONDON, even down to the riffraff, already knew what the ball's special announcement would be. There was no mystery, although The Dowager Duchess of Baynton's guests would feign surprise when the moment for the announcement arrived.

They called it the Match of the Century.

Her son, the Duke of Baynton, London's richest and unarguably most handsome gentleman, would announce his betrothal to Miss Elin Morris, also known as the Morris Heiress, thereby uniting two great fortunes and two magnificent adjoining country estates in Leicestershire along the River Trent.

And the reason everyone anticipated the "announcement" was because it was a well-known fact that Elin had been promised to the duke almost since the day of her birth. Yes, she had been presented at Court and had gone through the motions of a First Season, but it had all been just a formality, a "show." The duke was hers. She had Baynton, the epitome of a lordly lord, the Nonpareil.

"And I am not *worthy* of him," Elin whispered, stopping the furious pacing she'd been at for the last ten minutes in an attempt to settle anxious nerves and a confused mind.

Her bedroom in her parent's London house was fit for a princess. The India carpet in hues of blue was thick and soft beneath her stockinged feet. Her furniture was gilded in the opulent manner her parents preferred.

Back in Heartwood, the Morris family estate, which adjoined the Baynton's family seat, the furniture in her room was simple and to her tastes. Here, her parents ruled. They were London creatures, darlings of society known for their generosity and deep, abiding love for each other.

And Elin? Well, their only child preferred the quieter life at Heartwood. Of course, all that would change when she became Baynton's duchess. He was too important to have his wife rusticate in the country.

She caught a glimpse of herself in her dressing-table mirror, a lone figure in finely woven petticoats, her face pale beneath a mop of overcurly brown hair. Her dark eyes reflected her agitation. They threatened to swallow her face.

"It's not that I don't want Baynton," she attempted to explain to her image. "It is that I *shouldn't* have him. Not without telling him—"

Her bedroom door flew open, interrupting her thoughts, and her mother, Jennifer Morris, sparkling in the famed Morris diamonds, swept into the room. Her dress was of Belgian lace dyed in her favorite shade of sapphire, a color that matched her eyes. Her honey blond hair betrayed barely a trace of gray. She glowed with eagerness for the evening ahead. She enjoyed crowds and being the center of attention. She had looked forward to this night for over twenty years, ever since the old duke of Baynton had suggested a match between their children.

Jenny shut the door and took in the situation in the room—Elin in her petticoats, her hair curling without a sense of order or style—and focused on the supper tray on the desk by the window overlooking the back garden.

"What is this? You haven't touched any of your food. Sarah said she encouraged you to eat, but I can see you haven't taken even a bite." Her mother approached her. Jenny was half a head taller than her daughter. She cupped Elin's face in warm, loving hands. The rose scent of her perfume swirled around them. "Elin, you must eat. This evening is all about you. You are going to be very busy tonight. So many people will beg your attention, you won't have time to sit, let alone enjoy a bit of supper. Cook prepared the chicken in that French cream sauce you like so much. And then, sweet bee, you need to finish dressing. In fact, while you are eating, let me call for Sarah to do your hair. We don't want to keep Baynton and his guests waiting—"

Elin caught her mother's hand before she could move away. "I can't do this. I thought I could, but I can't."

"*You can,*" her mother answered. "You were meant to do this. Born for it. Elin—" She paused, closed her eyes as if searching for the right words, or patience. When she raised her lashes, her expression was one of loving concern. "Elin, forgive yourself. You made a mistake. It shouldn't have happened, but it did. However, it was many years ago. What were you, fifteen?"

"I was to turn sixteen."

"So very young. How could you have known? You trusted Benedict. Your father and I trusted him."

"I was foolish." A hard lump formed in Elin's chest at the mention of Benedict Whitridge's name. Ben had been her closest friend, and he had taken what she should have protected—her virginity. He was also her betrothed's youngest brother.

Not only had the experience been painful and humiliating, he'd gone away the very next day. He'd left for a career in the military without a word of farewell. Or a warning that he was leaving, that he wouldn't be there to reassure her when she needed him most.

Her mother led Elin to her dressing table. She gently pushed Elin to sit on the bench, then knelt on the carpet in front of her, taking her hands and holding them.

"My daughter, we have discussed this. I thought you'd forgiven yourself. It was not a good incident in your life, but nothing terrible came of it."

"I have forgiven myself." Elin's voice sounded false to her own ears. "I just believe Baynton should know."

"That his *brother* took advantage of his betrothed? Is that what you want to tell him?"

"I wouldn't say who." Especially since Baynton and his brothers had shared a turbulent history.

There had been three Whitridge sons residing at Baynton, until Gavin's twin, Jack, had disappeared one night from Eton. Some claimed he'd had run off. Others believed foul play. No matter which, he was never seen or heard from again.

The disappearance had meant that the old duke had not wanted to let his third son meet the same end. Or have the same opportunity to escape. The old duke had been an exacting taskmaster. He had high expectations for his heir. Ben often felt he was an afterthought. "A spare," Ben had always claimed, oftentimes bitterly. "Always kept at bay."

Because of Jack's disappearance, his father had kept him at Trenton, the family estate, and had him educated by a succession of tutors. Elin had been his sole companion.

As an only child of parents who were often in London, Elin had valued Ben's company. She'd trusted him and, to this day, could not believe he had taken her innocence to strike out at his oldest brother, as her mother had claimed. Then again, everyone knew the brothers were highly competitive. The old duke liked them that way.

However, to Elin, the loss of her purity was a small thing in the face of the betrayal of a trusted friend. She'd known he'd longed for independence. He'd yearned to buy his commission and set off into the world.

What she hadn't anticipated was that he would use her in such a deliberate way. That had seemed out of character. Her mother had assured her it was very much the nature of men and one of the reasons that, from now on, her parents would protect her more closely.

And so they had.

Elin was now three-and-twenty. Ben actually meant nothing to her save for a hard lesson learned.

She admitted to her mother, "Of the two brothers, I am marrying the best . . . but Baynton is known for his integrity. Is it wise to start a marriage with a deception?"

"And you could speak this honesty without telling the name of the man?" her mother repeated incredulously, then shook her head. "He would demand it or go mad with jealousy. Sweet bee, when a man's pride is on the line, he will move mountains to discover the truth. You know how single-minded your father can be."

Elin nodded. Fyclan Morris's story was well-known. He'd been an Irish nobody who had raised himself to the highest levels of society.

"Well, Baynton is even more so. Your honesty could destroy any chance you have at a happy marriage. He will not cry off. His honor won't let him. And this means so much to your father."

The marriage also meant a great deal to her mother as well. Jenny Tarleton had married beneath her.

Fyclan had been a man full of big dreams and confidence. He'd told her that his children's were to someday be dukes and princes. His Romney grandmother had foretold it, and if Jenny ran away with him, if she eloped against her family's wishes, she would have no regrets.

And now, Fyclan was now one of the most respected businessmen in London. Certainly, he was the wealthiest. Through Elin, the prophecy was about to be fulfilled.

"I know what this marriage means to you and Papa,"

Elin said as gently as she could. "However, I feel it only fair to tell Baynton of my indiscretion. I was foolish."

Her mother leaned forward. "My darling daughter, there isn't a woman alive who hasn't been foolish at one time or the other. You took it too far, but the simple truth is, you are not the first woman to go to her husband's bed after having lost her purity to another, and you will not be the last."

Elin knew this was true. She'd heard the other young women of her acquaintance whispering.

"Benedict is gone," her mother continued. "He is far away serving on some battlefield, plumping his vanity. He wanted to hurt his brother, and if you do tell Baynton what happened, then he will have succeeded."

For a moment, Elin sat silent. Then she pulled her hands from her mother's grip and turned on the bench to face her image in the mirror. Her expression had lost its haunted look. She lifted her chin with resolve. "Will you send for Sarah? I need to dress."

"Are you going to make a confession to Baynton?" Her mother rose to her feet.

"There isn't any sense to it, is there?"

Her mother kissed her on the top of her unruly curls. "Only the future matters, sweet bee. Baynton will make you a wonderful husband. Your son will be magnificent. Yes, I'll fetch Sarah, and don't forget to manage a bite or two."

She started for the door, but Elin had one last question, something she'd always wondered knowing how close her parents were. "Does Father know what happened between Ben and me?"

Her mother stopped at the door, one hand ready to turn the handle. "Men are not as wise about these matters as we women are. He would have called Benedict out. It would not do for a grown man to duel a seventeen-year-old boy."

She opened the door. "This is your night. Do not fear your destiny. Let this evening be one filled with the joy of an open heart. And when you walk into Menheim"—she referred to the Baynton's London home—"look toward the sitting room because someday soon, your portrait, the portrait of a young duchess, will grace the mantel there. The pictures of your children will line the walls around you. And Baynton will value you above all others." On those words, she left the room with perfumed grace.

Elin confronted herself in the looking glass. Since that fateful night, she'd lived a circumspect life. "My son will be a duke," she whispered, testing the words that filled her parents with confidence, and yet, she felt nothing.

However, when all was said and done, the least she could do was to please her parents, to make them happy. Baynton was a good man. She didn't know him well because he was so incredibly important, he was busy all the time, but she liked his mother. She respected Marcella and prayed she was half as dignified and good of heart as the Dowager.

A knock sounded on the door, and Sarah entered the room to help Elin dress.

FEW WOMEN WERE as energetic as Marcella, The Dowager Duchess of Baynton. She was ten years Jennifer Morris's senior, but she appeared young enough to be her contemporary.

The Dowager's jewels of choice for the evening were her blood red garnets. They circled her throat, her wrists, and her fingers and stood out against silvery gray of her dress. In her white-blond hair, she wore a bandeau in garnet red. She appeared queenly and gracious, as was her welcome for her dearest friends in the upstairs sitting room reserved for family. They were not alone. The room was crowded with Baynton's relatives, some of whom Elin knew, but many she did not. The sound of the musicians tuning their instruments drifted up the stairs from the ballroom.

"Jenny, you are radiant," Her Grace said in greeting. "And, dear Fyclan, how handsome."

Elin's father did look good. He might not have been as tall as his wife, but there was a presence about him that made others take notice. Elin had gained the exotic shape of her brown eyes as well as her dark hair from him . His hair, once been as black as a raven's wing, was now silver.

Surprisingly, the years had been unkind to him. He used a walking cane now and not just for effect. Elin and her mother both worried after him. He was a man who worked far too hard.

However, tonight was one for celebration. Fyclan offered the duchess the kiss of friendship. "You are stunning as well, Your Grace."

Marcella laughed, an expression that quickly took a dangerous turn toward tears. She pressed a gloved hand to her cheek. "I'm so sorry, Fyclan, it is nothing you said.

My husband had so anticipated this evening and to a wedding between our two families. You know how highly he thought of you?"

"I do, and I miss his friendship daily."

"Yes," the Dowager agreed and sent a sad smile in Elin's direction. "And here I haven't even told you how lovely you are, my Elin. You look like a young Helen of Troy," she declared. "The pale peach of that dress sets your skin off to perfection. Your mother and I knew it would when we saw it, and I so admire the bands of gold holding your curls."

Elin blushed with the compliment. But before she could respond, the duchess said quietly, "You and Gavin should have been married years ago. I feel so much regret over what happened."

Jenny rested a hand on her friend's shoulder. "My dear, it isn't your fault that your husband took ill. The marriage could wait until he was better."

"But he never became better." Again the duchess's eyes misted over the loss of her beloved husband. Elin and Gavin were to have been betrothed four years earlier, but the duke's illness and subsequent death, not to mention the challenges Gavin faced in assuming the duties of the title, had set back plans for a wedding.

"I'm sorry," Marcella apologized, taking a kerchief a footman offered and dabbing her cheeks, "for being a watering pot. I must stop this, or I will not make it through the night."

"We all understand how difficult it is," Elin's mother assured her.

"But John would have expected better of me." Marcella gathered herself with a sigh. "Here, I have not offered you anything in the way of refreshment—" she started but was interrupted by the appearance of her son in the doorway.

All the attention in the room went to *him.*

Gavin Whitridge, the Duke of Baynton, bounded into the room with his mother's energy. He was over six feet tall and had a smile that melted hearts. Dressed in his evening finest, he cut a figure that every dandy on the morrow would attempt to emulate and fail because the Duke of Baynton was truly that unique. That remarkable. That masculine.

He was known for his deep blue eyes, broad shoulders, square jaw, and the most perfect straight nose ever to grace a man's face. His thick hair was as black as night.

He was so completely an astonishing specimen of male beauty, Elin always felt a bit intimidated.

The crush of relatives moved forward, anxious to claim his attention, but then fell back when they realized he was searching for someone. His keen gaze fell on Elin.

He moved directly toward her. His gaze slid over her with appreciation, and he smiled. He liked her. He was pleased, and she was surprised at how his open admiration helped to settle her frayed nerves.

Gavin was nine years older than her and had thrown himself tirelessly into the duties of being a duke. Before his father's death, he'd been expected to deal with the minor responsibilities that had still kept him very busy. There had been times when he'd escorted her family to events, but the two of them had few opportunities to just talk or to relax around each other. There were expectations, just as there was now.

"You are beautiful," he said, his voice low. He held out his hand.

Elin found it hard to meet the intensity in his eyes. She offered him her gloved hand, but instead of bowing over it or even pressing a kiss to her fingers, he took her hand fully in his own. "Come." He started to cut through his relatives, pulling her toward the door

"Baynton," his mother said, "where do you believe you are going? We need to start the receiving line. And you haven't said a word of welcome to anyone else."

He laughed, the sound strong and sure. "Welcome," he announced with a wave as he continued guiding Elin to the door. "Go downstairs without us, Mother. We shall be there momentarily. I promise"

On those words, he hurried Elin across the hall to a wood paneled library. The room was cozy and apparently also served as his office. The sounds of musicians beginning to play could not be heard here.

Baynton closed the door.

Self-conscious Elin walked toward the desk. The walls were lined with overstuffed bookshelves. No wonder sound couldn't penetrate his sanctuary. There was a gilded clock on the mantel and a crystal-and-gilt inkpot and pen on the desk.

"Elin, face me."

She did as he requested.

Solemnly they studied each other. The anxiousness churning inside her began to slow.

He moved first, walking toward her, stopping when there was barely a foot between them. She had to tilt her head back to look at him. Seeing her do so, he sat on the edge of a leather upholstered the chair, the sort men favored, to bring himself down more to her height.

"Are you ready for this, Elin?"

The question startled her. Did he have doubts? "I believe so, Your Grace—"

"Gavin. Call me Gavin." There was a beat of silence, filled only by the ticking of the mantel clock. Then, he said, "We are to be man and wife. I've waited for this time. I've longed for it."

She wanted to tell him that she'd waited for this moment as well, but shyness caught the words in her throat. Yes, shyness and also a bit of hope. What he was doing was good. Caring. She could love a caring man. She could love *him*.

And he wanted her.

Besides admiration there was an eagerness about him. An adorableness. She'd never seen this side of him or had ever imagined that he *wanted* to marry her. She had assumed his was nothing more than an obligation, an honorable one, but an obligation dictated by his father all the same.

Just as she'd been dictated to by her parents . . . however, now, her feelings shifted.

Elin kept such thoughts close. It was too soon for declarations of any sort.

Ben came to her mind . . . Ben and what she'd once believed was between them.

Gavin was not Ben, but let *him* be the vulnerable one, then she would know she was safe.

He didn't seem to be put off by her reserve. Instead, he gifted her with another of those smiles, this one making her almost sway with dizziness over how blinding it was. He pulled a velvet pouch from the inside of his black evening dress jacket.

"My father gave this necklace to my mother." He opened the pouch and poured into his hands a string of creamy pearls. "He said it had once belonged to Mary Stuart. His intent was that it be worn by the brides of Baynton. Would you honor me and my family by accepting this gift and wearing it this evening?" He stood, setting the pouch on the chair and holding the necklace out to place it around her throat. "May I?"

Now Elin truly was speechless. She had never seen anything lovelier than these pearls. How could she have had doubts about this man? This marriage?

And she felt ashamed that she'd wasted her virginity, the only thing that had been truly hers to give to her husband, on the wrong man. Tears filled her eyes.

Even though she blinked them back, Gavin noticed immediately. "What have I done? Have I made you unhappy? You don't have to wear the necklace—" He acted as if he would throw it back in the pouch.

Elin stayed his hand, catching him at the wrist. Her actions brought her closer to him. Her skirts brushed his legs. She could feel his body heat. His shaving soap was spicy, masculine. She liked it.

"The necklace is beautiful, Gavin. I'm just touched by your generosity. You honor me. You honor my family." And the latter meant more to her than the former.

"You are to be my wife. I mean to honor you," he said. His gallant words went directly to her heart even as his gaze shifted from her eyes down to her mouth.

She found her lips suddenly dry, too dry for a kiss, and she moistened them . . . an invitation.

He smiled. This time, his smile was not blinding, but admiring. When he looked at her like this, she really did feel lovely. "We are going to do very well together, Elin," he promised. "I'm going to kiss you."

"I know." Her voice had gone low and husky.

"Good," he replied. He drew a breath and leaned toward her. Their closed lips met, brushed against each other, held sweetly for a second, then he drew back. Elin wanted to follow. Her breasts skimmed the material of his jacket, as her hand reached for his lapel for support. That was not enough of a kiss. *More*, she wanted more. That tiny kiss did nothing save stir long-forgotten fires inside her . . . *fires she had once discovered with Ben—*

The door to the library flew open and crashed against the wall.

The duke and Elin both jumped in surprise. Gavin placed himself between Elin and the door, the pearls still in his hands.

"Your Grace," Sawyer, the Menheim butler was babbling from the hallway, "I am sorry you are bothered. I tried to stop him. He refused to listen to me."

"Stop *me?*" the uninvited guest repeated. "From seeing my own *beloved* brother?" There was no love in that hard tone.

Brother? It couldn't be. Elin bent to see around Baynton.

It *was* him.

Benedict Whitridge, Lord Ben as he was known around Menheim, or Major Whitridge in his other life, stood in the doorway, his uniform disheveled by travel and his manner one of such anger, he appeared ready to launch himself at his brother.

But those were only surface changes.

Elin found herself shocked by the deeper changes. He was taller than his brother now and his shoulders as broad except that he had retained the lean physique and long muscular thighs of the horseman he'd once been. There were lines at the corners of his eyes as if he'd spent hours squinting into the sun or laughing. The smooth skin of his boyhood had given way to a day's growth of beard along the line of his hard jaw.

And his brows were thicker, more animated. Elin had always enjoyed Ben's brows because they said louder than words exactly what was going on in his mind. Right now, they punctuated the vivid intelligence in eyes that were a lighter hue from the duke's.

Of the two brothers, Gavin was definitely the more classically handsome. Still, each was the sort of man whose presence could fill a room.

However, while Baynton was known *for* his sterling character, Elin remembered how Ben had charmed her *with* his character, his humor, his witticisms over comings and goings of those around them. He'd made her laugh.

Until the day he didn't.

Until the day he'd broken her young, trusting heart.

Gavin tucked the pearls into his pocket. "It is all right, Sawyer. Please see to my guests. And as for you, *brother*, we will discuss anything you wish *later*. Right now, I am expected downstairs." He spoke with the cool dismissal of a man accustomed to being obeyed.

In answer, Ben slammed the door shut. "Your guests will wait, *brother*. We talk *now*."

About the Author

CATHY MAXWELL spends hours in front of her computer pondering the question, "Why do people fall in love?" It remains for her the great mystery of life and the secret to happiness. She lives in beautiful Virginia with children, horses, dogs, and cats. Fans can contact Cathy at www.cathymaxwell.com or PO Box 1135, Powhatan, VA 23139.

Discover great authors, exclusive offers, and more at hc.com.